Totally Bound Publi

Bo
To Lov
To Lo
To Lo

CW00486201

Boundaries

TO LOVE AND OBEY

KATY SWANN

To Love and Obey
ISBN # 978-1-78184-737-4
©Copyright Katy Swann 2014
Cover Art by Posh Gosh ©Copyright January 2014
Interior text design by Claire Siemaszkiewicz
Totally Bound Publishing

Published in 2014 by Totally Bound Publishing, Newland House, The Point, Weaver Road, Lincoln, LN6 3QN, United Kingdom.

Totally Bound Publishing is an imprint of Total-E-Ntwined Limited.

TO LOVE AND OBEY

Dedication

Thank you to my friends, family and fellow authors for all your support and encouragement. And thank you to Totally Bound for giving me a chance to tell Rachel and Adam's story.

Chapter One

Rachel Porter stared out at the London skyline and sighed. She was sitting in Adam Stone's chair in his plush office, daydreaming about the day before. It had been Sunday and she'd spent the whole weekend with Adam. And what a weekend it had been.

She shuddered as she recalled Dominique's attack on Saturday night and her hateful words as she'd bitterly told Rachel that she was, in fact, Adam's wife. Well, ex-wife, but that little fact wasn't going to stop Dominique from getting Adam back as far as she was concerned.

Rachel moved slightly and flinched as the remaining pain from Dominique's vicious whips stung her back. Thank God Adam had gotten to her before Dominique had carried out her threat and torn her skin off. Rachel had passed out in his arms when he'd found her, and she had woken up in his bed several hours later.

She ran her hand over the smooth, polished mahogany of Adam's desk and smiled. He was in Birmingham today for a conference, and as she was up to date with all her work, she'd decided to enjoy the view from his office. This was where she'd first come face to face with him. God, he'd intimated her then.

She could, of course, catch up with the pile of filing hidden under her desk, but somehow she didn't find that idea very appealing. What Adam didn't know, wouldn't hurt him and if he should find the pile, what could he do? Punish her? *Yes, please.*

She thought back to the day before—it had been one of those days that had left her stunned. Adam had drawn the most beautiful picture of her kneeling, naked and aroused, on the floor of his studio. He had then fucked her hard before showing her the picture he'd just drawn and that was when the persistent niggle of doubt had returned.

He had drawn a collar around her neck—the sort only twenty-four-seven slaves wore, and had then told her that he would collar her permanently, one way or another. And what had she done? Instead of telling him there and then that she didn't want to be his slave, she had changed the subject and muttered something about needing to get home.

Why couldn't she just have told him how she felt? She knew why, though. If he knew she wouldn't agree, he'd probably leave her and find someone that could meet his needs. The thought of losing him was inconceivable.

Suddenly, the phone in her office rang, snapping Rachel back to the view in front of her. She jumped up then quickly ran to her desk, grabbing the phone just before it diverted to the main reception.

"Rachel Porter. Can I help you?" She hoped it was Adam.

"Rach? It's Vicky from downstairs." Vicky was one of her old colleagues when she'd worked for Joe. The day Adam had demanded that she come and work for him, Joe had been furious and Vicky and the gang had been deeply sympathetic. No one had envied her new job — Adam Stone had a reputation for being as demanding as he was ruthless. Most people, herself included, hadn't expected her to last more than a couple of days before getting fired.

"Hi, Vicky. How are you?" She liked Vicky, but she hardly saw any of the old gang anymore. Once you worked on the executive floor, it seemed you became one of the 'unreachables' and it had taken a while for her to get used to being treated differently by her old peers. She'd felt lonely, cut-off and had hated her new job, including Adam, in the beginning.

"We heard that the boss is out of town so the girls and I wondered if you fancied coming to lunch with us?" piped Vicky in her high-pitched, friendly voice.

Rachel swallowed a lump in her throat. She really missed the lunches with the girls.

"I'd love to," she said, smiling into the handset.

"Great. Meet us in reception in five minutes," said Vicky then hung up.

So, they hadn't forgotten about her. She got up, made sure Adam's chair was exactly as he'd left it and hurried to the ladies to touch up her makeup.

Ten minutes later, she was sitting in the local café with six of the girls from her old office. They were all chatting and laughing at once, sharing office gossip and teasing Stacey about fancying one of the guys from IT Support. It was just like old times, she'd missed this camaraderie.

After they had all ordered their food, Bianca, the girl who had taken over her old job, had a moan about Joe being so untidy. Rachel smiled to herself as she listened. Joe was the pole opposite of Adam.

"So, Rach," said Vicky, as the waitress brought their food. "How come Mr Stone hasn't fired you yet?"

Rachel laughed. "Oh thanks. I'm not that bad."

All the girls raised their eyebrows, and Rachel grinned, enjoying their good-natured ribbing.

"What's he like, then?" asked Bridget, one of the admin assistants, with wide eyes. "Is he really as bad as they say?"

"Oh, worse," replied Rachel, her face deadpan. "Much worse. If I make a mistake he puts me over his knee and spanks me."

The girls erupted into fits of giggles at Rachel's 'joke' and waited for her to continue. Rachel shrugged. "There's not really much to tell, to be honest. He's demanding, but fair. The fact I still have a job is testament to that."

"Well, rather you than me," said Vicky, dipping a chip in a big splodge of ketchup. "He may be gorgeous, but he looks like he might eat you alive."

Rachel giggled. "Oh, yes. He does that as well." If only they knew.

Stacey coughed to get everyone's attention then lowered her voice. "I've heard he's into weird things. You know, kinky stuff."

The girls all laughed and told her not to be so ridiculous, but Stacey was adamant. "No, really. Apparently he owns some dodgy club or something. My mate's sister went out with a guy who'd been there. It's full of whips and chains and stuff."

All six heads turned to look at Rachel, and she couldn't help the blush that rose from her neck and crept into her cheeks.

"Well, Rach?" asked Bridget. "Do you know anything about that?"

Rachel decided to play dumb. "For God's sake," she said, grinning, "I'm only his bloody PA. How would I know what he gets up to in private?" She knew he wasn't too bothered about keeping Boundaries a secret. After all, it was hardly illegal. But she wasn't about to confirm or deny anything, so she kept quiet.

"Well, I think he's gorgeous, whether he's into weird stuff, or not," sighed Stacey.

"Yeah, you and every female employee at Stone Media," said Vicky, grinning.

"He's got a body to die for, don't you think?" Stacey looked at Rachel as she spoke.

"Really?" said Rachel, with a nonchalant shrug. "I hadn't noticed."

Luckily, the conversation then moved on to more mundane office gossip and the rest of the lunch break was spent catching up with what everyone was up to in their busy lives. All too soon, lunch was over and it was time to head back to the office. As the group made their way back, Rachel's mobile phone rang so she hung discreetly back and checked the display. It was Adam.

"Hi," she said, as quietly as she could.

"Hello, sexy."

His voice sent a little shiver down her spine.

"What are you up to?" he asked.

She glanced at Vicky and the other girls, all in deep conversation and replied, quietly, "I've been to lunch with the girls."

"Did you have a nice time?"

"Yes, thanks, I did. How's the conference?"

"Boring. I miss you," he said, his voice deep and husky.

She grinned. God, if the girls only knew. "You only saw me yesterday," she giggled.

"I still miss you. Call me when you're back in the office. Make sure you're alone." Was that a hint of Dom in his voice?

"Okay." She wasn't about to call him Sir in front of the girls, even if they didn't know who she was talking to. She hung up and rejoined the conversation, as they strolled back to work.

Once back in the office, Rachel closed the outer door to her office and dialed Adam's number on her mobile. He answered immediately.

"Are you alone?" Yep, there was definitely a sexy dose of Dom in his voice.

"Yes, Sir," she replied, as her stomach fluttered with excitement. God, he wasn't even there and he still had the power to make her insides melt.

"Good. Now, go into my office, open the third drawer down in my desk and take out the box at the back of the drawer."

What the hell was he up to? She did as he'd said, and when she'd found the box, she told him so.

"Good. Now, go into the boardroom, lock the door and strip."

Strip? Had he just told her to strip in the fucking boardroom? "Adam…"

"Wrong answer," he snapped. Even though she couldn't see him, she knew he was frowning.

She sighed. "Yes, Sir." Oh boy, this was going to be an interesting afternoon.

She tentatively made her way to the boardroom, locked the door, double checking it to make sure it really was locked, then turned to face the windows. Oh, God, there was an office building directly adjacent. Why hadn't she noticed that before? What if someone saw her through the window? Bit late for that, she thought as a memory replayed itself in her head. She'd been bent over the table as Adam had spanked her. Hard. She felt herself moisten at the memory.

"What are you thinking about, Rachel?"

"Er... Well, I was thinking about the building opposite, Sir." She blushed at the thought of anyone seeing her.

"And?"

Bloody hell. Did he know what she had been thinking?

"And about the time you spanked me in here, Sir."

She heard him chuckle and couldn't help smiling as she pictured him standing over her, arms on his hips, ready to master her.

"Are you naked yet?"

What? "But, Adam...Sir... What if someone in the other building sees?" she stammered. Surely he wouldn't...?

"Screw them," he growled. "They'll get an afternoon treat. If I have to say it again, Rachel, I will punish you."

The word 'punish' was all it took to send a little electric shock down to her pussy, but before she'd had a chance to process the feeling, Adam spoke again, "Don't even think about it. You wouldn't enjoy this punishment. Trust me."

How the hell did he know her so well?

"Okay, Sir. I'm undressing now." As she hastily unbuttoned her blouse and pulled it open to expose her bare breasts, she glanced nervously at the window. There were two men sitting at their desks near the big wall of glass. Their backs were turned, but all it would take was...

"Are you ready?" Adam sounded impatient now.

"Nearly, Sir," she said, as she hurriedly slipped her skirt down and stepped out of it, leaving her naked, except for her shoes. Adam had forbidden her to wear underwear to the office. "Okay, Sir. Ready."

"Is anyone looking at you from the opposite building?" he asked.

She looked again. Luckily, they were still facing away from the window. "No, Sir," she replied, through gritted teeth.

"Shame."

Bastard! As Rachel stood in the boardroom, completely naked and exposed to anyone who might look across from the other building, she felt an overwhelming sense of shame. And arousal. Damn, how could she be getting turned on by the thought of someone seeing her naked?

Then Adam spoke again, leaving her in no doubt as to his intentions, "Lie down on the table. Put your phone on speaker and leave it next to you. Spread your legs and imagine that I've tied them to the corners of the table."

"But…"

"Do it. *Now!*"

Oh, God. If she'd ever wanted to die of shame, it was now. She climbed slowly onto the table, never taking her eyes off the window, put her phone on speaker and slowly spread her legs.

The cool breeze from the air conditioning brushed against her damp pussy, reminding her that she wasn't normal. How could anyone get turned on by the risk of getting caught like this? What if someone across the road took a picture? *Shit.*

"Pick up your phone and hold it above you. Take a picture of yourself and email it to me."

"Adam Stone, you are one sick perv," she groaned as she picked up the phone. And to think that less than half an hour ago, she'd been pretending she knew nothing about his kinky habits.

She stuck her tongue out and took a picture, which she quickly emailed to him. Within seconds she heard Adam's approval.

"Good girl. You look gorgeous. I wish I was there now." His voice was soft, sexy.

"So do I, Sir," she whispered and closed her eyes. God, how she wished he was there with her now. Then he'd be just as fucking likely to get caught.

"Touch yourself, Rachel. Are you wet?" A memory from Hampstead Heath sprung to her mind, and she shuddered.

She slipped her hand between her outstretched legs and ran a finger along the opening to her pussy. She was soaked.

"Yes, Sir. I'm wet."

"Good. Now, with one hand I want you to play with your breasts. Pull and squeeze your nipples, I want to hear groans of pain. With your other hand, I want you to fuck yourself. You may use as many fingers as you like," he added, with a chuckle.

"Oh, how kind of you, Sir," she snapped, and reluctantly obeyed.

As she probed her damp entrance with her fingers, she wanted to know if he was just as turned on. "Permission to ask a question, Sir," she said, trying to sound as normal as possible.

"Go on."

"You asked if I'm wet. Are you hard, Sir?"

The sound of his laugh rang through the boardroom and she grinned. How she loved that laugh.

"Yes, sweet thing. Rock hard."

Good, although she'd bet he wasn't splayed out on a table in front of a bloody window.

"Fuck yourself, Rachel. I want to hear you."

There was only one thing for it. She closed her eyes and imagined Adam standing over her, fully dressed in his Dom's leathers. She envisioned a flogger in one hand and his hard cock in the other.

She pinched a nipple and groaned as the pain sent a little bolt of sensation down between her legs. She pinched harder then pulled on the nub, which was now hard and engorged. She thought about Adam's face, watching her, waiting for just the right moment to plunge himself deep inside her.

She used two fingers to pleasure herself with, every now and again bringing them out to rub against her clit. Unbelievably, she almost forgot where she was as she imagined Adam's flogger draping over her body. She could almost feel the soft leather fronds tickling her. She groaned.

"Stop!"

Huh? Had she just heard right?

"Rachel. Did you hear me? I said stop," said Adam, brusquely.

She almost growled her reply, "Yes, Sir."

"Are you horny?"

"Yes, Sir."

"Do you want to come?"

"Yes, Sir."

"Well, you can't. You do not have permission to come. Do you understand?"

"Yes, Sir," she hissed. Her hand was still between her legs. All it would take would be a little…

"Good. Now sit up, slide over to the edge of the table and climb off. Oh, and make sure you climb off on the window side."

No way! She turned her head and to her horror, saw two people standing right by the window opposite. They were deep in conversation, but if one were to glance out...

Shame burned through her body and, for the first time, she considered using her safe word.

"Rachel? Did you hear me?" Adam's insistent voice reminded her of how much she wanted to please him. He wouldn't be happy if she chickened out by safe wording when, to be honest, it wasn't really necessary. She knew he respected her right to use her safe word, it wasn't that, but she also knew that he expected her to use her best judgment and only use it if she really couldn't cope with a situation. And to be fair she could cope with this, no matter how uncomfortable it made her feel.

"Yes, Sir, I heard but... Sir? There's someone standing right by the window."

"Are they looking out?" he asked.

"Well, no. Not right now, but..."

"In that case, do as I say. You'll just have to hope they're too engrossed in their conversation to notice a naked woman in the window opposite them." Adam's voice didn't give anything away, except for one thing. He was serious.

It occurred to her that she could just slip discreetly off the table and hide on the floor where no one would see her. After all, Adam wasn't there to check. He'd never know. But she would, and she knew that he would work it out. He was so damned perceptive.

So she gritted her teeth, sat up and slid toward the edge of the table. As she climbed down, one of the people opposite turned their head and Rachel instinctively ducked down. She waited a moment or two then peeped up to check that the coast was clear. The man had looked away again. Thank God.

"What are you doing, Rachel?"

"Standing by the window like you said, Sir," replied Rachel with a slightly brittle edge to her voice. She couldn't help it—this was just too bloody embarrassing. So why was she so turned on?

"Good girl," he said.

The approval in his voice confused her body. What was more important? Adam's approval, or her modesty? *Damn him.*

"Get the box you took out of my drawer and open it."

When she opened the box, she groaned. She knew what was coming next.

"Take the bullet vibrator out and insert it into your vagina."

Jesus, he was going to make her wear a bloody vibrator for the rest of the day. Well, the one advantage she had was that he wasn't there to activate it. Small comfort, but still... The bullet slipped in easily thanks to her being so wet from pleasuring herself. She wondered if there was a little switch on it. He'd never know if she experimented a little and...

"Is it in?"

"Yes, Sir."

"Good. Now listen carefully. Don't even think of trying to activate it yourself, there are no controls on it. It's connected to my mobile phone using Bluetooth. Only I can activate it." He sounded smug, as if he knew what she'd been thinking.

Rachel shook her head. A phone activated vibrator? Whatever next?

Adam continued, "I want you to keep your phone next to you all afternoon. Every time it bleeps with a text, the vibrator will be activated. You will not come. Understood?"

"Yeah," she groaned. "*Sir.*"

"Good. You may get dressed now."

Rachel was just about to move away from the window, when he added, "In front of the window."

She scowled at the phone. Should she move away? Damn him, but she couldn't disobey him, he had her over a barrel.

When she was dressed, Adam spoke again, "I want to test the vibrator. Brace yourself." A moment later, her phone vibrated, alerting her to the fact that she had a text. A second after that, the bullet sprang to life and she groaned as powerful vibrations stirred up her earlier arousal.

"Ahhh," she cried, and clenched her legs together.

"Good, I hear it's working. Excellent. Remember, do not come at any time."

"Yes, Sir," she growled, her legs buckling slightly as the strong sensations buzzed through her body. She silently cursed the vibrator, it was bloody powerful. How on earth was she going to control herself with this thing going off intermittently and unexpectedly?

"By the way. The windows are covered with a special reflective film, they're one-way. No one can see in." He laughed at her gasp. "Oh, and Rachel?"

"Yes, Sir?"

"I love you."

The phone went dead and she was left staring at the window in disbelief. He'd made her suffer by letting her think that anyone looking in would be able to see her. She smiled as she realized that she should have known he wouldn't have put her in such a compromising position. She grinned and unlocked the door. The vibrator had thankfully stopped again, but she couldn't ignore the reminder of its presence as she sat down on her chair.

She sighed. This was going to be a long afternoon.

Chapter Two

An hour passed with no activity. The phone only rang once and Rachel was bored. She'd even done some of the filing. She didn't dare go on the Internet, even for non-kinky stuff, knowing that IT kept an eye on all employees' internet activity.

She played a game of solitaire on her computer and was so engrossed that she didn't notice her phone bleep. The vibrator sprang to life, making her jump with shock. She'd actually forgotten about it. A few seconds later, her mobile rang. Adam's name on the caller ID told her he was going to torment her some more.

"Hello, gorgeous," he purred through the earpiece.

"Hello, Sir." The vibrations were very strong and it didn't take long before the familiar first sensations of arousal stirred back up inside her.

"Are you alone?"

"Yes, Sir." She groaned as the vibrations increased.

"Good. Close your eyes and imagine yourself kneeling naked in front of me."

She closed her eyes and listened to the velvet tones of his voice seducing her.

"What can you see in your mind, Rachel?"

Oh, yes. A shudder ran through her body as she imagined herself kneeling, naked, before him in his office, like an offering to be used for his pleasure.

"I see you standing in front of me, Sir. You're wearing your black leather boots and leather trousers." The more the vision became real, the more the vibrations inside her pussy aroused her.

"Good girl. Now reach down and touch yourself, but don't come."

Her clit was starting to throb in time with the vibrations and she wasn't sure she would be able to stop herself from coming if she touched herself. But she needed to obey Adam, so she opened her legs, reached down and pushed her fingers between her warm thighs. She groaned as she rubbed them against her pulsing clit. She knew release wasn't far away. The need was still lingering from her time in the boardroom. She pressed a bit harder and her muscles tightened. *Oh, yes. Nearly there.*

"Don't come, Rachel."

Adam's voice abruptly brought her back down and she quickly removed her hand to make sure she wouldn't come.

"Tell me how you feel," he said.

"I...I want you to fuck me. I'm wet, Adam. Wet, for you. Please let me come." She knew she was whining, but she couldn't help it. Her earlier denial was making it so much harder this time.

"Not yet." His voice was unsympathetic and uncompromising.

The vibrations stopped just after he rang off and Rachel was left with an empty ache. She tried to get back to her solitaire, but she was restless and distracted. Her pussy was still wet and the ache just wouldn't go away. Sitting down only made her more aware of the bullet so she ended up pacing the floor reciting the times tables as a distraction.

Nothing worked. She was horny, agitated and frustrated. And bloody close to giving in to temptation. Adam would never know if she snuck into the boardroom and played with her clit just enough to take the edge off. But she knew she couldn't lie to him. Apart from the fact that he'd see right through her, she would feel so guilty that he'd know something was up.

So she gritted her teeth and continued to pace until she heard her phone bleep. *Oh shit.* She rushed back to her desk, ready to grab the phone when Adam rang, and braced herself for the vibrations to start. But nothing happened. She was almost disappointed.

She picked up the phone and glared at it, her frustration making her cack-handed as she keyed in her password. It was only a text from Mandy. She asked if she'd be home tonight because Dawn was coming and would she like to join them for dinner? She quickly replied that she'd love to and put the phone down again.

She had to wait another agonizing twenty minutes before her phoned beeped again. This time, the vibrations did start and, like before, shortly after, it rang.

"Have you touched yourself?" Adam wasted no time in getting to the point.

"No, Sir," she growled. Thank God she'd abstained.

"Good girl."

The vibrations reignited her arousal so quickly that her legs weakened and she had to sit down quickly before they buckled. Unfortunately that only made the vibrations feel stronger and she closed her eyes as she tried to hold onto what little self-control she had left.

"Rachel?" Adam's voice sounded impatient. He'd asked her something.

"Oh, sorry. What did you say, Sir?"

"I asked what you're thinking right now."

She practically spat her reply out, "I'm thinking that you're a sadistic bastard. *Sir!*"

She heard him chuckle and at that moment, she almost hated him.

"Close your eyes and imagine being draped over my lap with your bare arse ready for my hand."

That wasn't hard. As she pictured herself bent over his lap, she slipped her hand between her legs without thinking. She groaned as her finger made contact with her aching clit.

"Are you touching yourself?"

She quickly snapped her hand away and almost cried with frustration as her body protested. "No, Sir." Not anymore, anyway.

"I think you're lying, Rachel. I was going to let you come, but I've changed my mind. Touching yourself without permission and lying is cause for punishment, Rachel."

His voice teased her. He knew what her reaction to his words would be.

"Oh, please, Sir. I beg you. Let me come. *Pleeease.*"

But he ignored her desperate pleas and changed the subject. "How are you getting home tonight?"

Oh God, no. "Bus, Sir," she stammered.

"Text me when you're on the bus." The phone went dead and Rachel was left staring at it in disbelief. The bus?

How was she going to make it through the afternoon? It wouldn't have been quite so bad if she'd had plenty of work to keep her distracted, but she didn't. Even her filing was up to date.

Finally, at five o'clock, she grabbed her bag and left, clenching her pelvic floor muscles tightly so as not to drop the bullet.

She boarded her bus and found a seat as far away from the majority of the passengers as possible. Snuggling up against the window, she texted Adam.

On bus.

She knew what was coming next. Sure enough, seconds later the phone bleeped followed quickly by the bullet coming back to life. Oh, God, she didn't know how many more times she could hold off. She was close. So close.

The phone rang and she quickly answered before she drew too much attention to herself.

"Hello?" As if she didn't know who it was.

"Are you wet for me, Rachel?"

Jesus, he doesn't waste any time.

"Yes, Sir," she replied quietly.

"Tell me. I want to hear you say it."

"Adam, I'm on the bloody bus," she snapped.

"Say it," he snapped back.

Bloody hell, this was like a bad dream. An erotic bad dream. "Yes, I'm wet for you, Sir," she practically whispered.

"Good girl. Now, imagine you can have my cock inside you, anywhere you like. Where would you like my cock?" His voice sounded so normal that he could have been asking what she'd like for dinner.

She didn't have to think twice about the answer. "In my mouth, Sir," she replied as quietly as she could.

"Pardon? Can you say that again?"

"I'd like your cock in my mouth, Sir," she practically growled. She didn't dare look around to see if anyone had heard.

"Okay. Keep your eyes closed and focus on the vibrations in your pussy. Now, imagine yourself kneeling, naked, in front of me, just like before. Now imagine yourself reaching up for my cock with your hands."

She did and her pussy contracted painfully.

"Now," continued Adam, "imagine putting your lips around the head of my cock. Lick it, taste it, suck it."

She smiled as she visualized his cock in her mouth. Oh, yes. Her clit started throbbing again and she clenched her hands as her pent-up frustrations came surging back. She felt his cock deep in her throat as he thrust it in, fucking her mouth as if it were her...

"Argh," she cried, almost forgetting where she was.

Adam's voice sounded deep and husky when he spoke again. He was clearly enjoying this as well. "When you think I'm about to come inside your mouth, you may come."

All she heard were the words, 'you may come' and her whole body stiffened as her muscles contracted in response to the intense fire burning between her legs. She quickly clamped a hand over her mouth and tried not to cry out as wave after excruciating wave crashed through her.

Her earlier denials were making this so much more intense, and she longed to scream out her release. Then, her body spasmed with aftershocks almost as powerful as the main eruption.

Finally, her body calmed and reality came back to her with agonizing clarity. Shit, she'd just had a major fucking orgasm on the bloody bus. She looked around her, but no one was taking any notice. Luckily there was another bus right ahead of them so hers wasn't as busy as it might have been. There was no one sitting next to her and she silently thanked God for the small mercy.

Thankfully, the vibrations stopped then and her equilibrium was slowly restored as her body returned to normal.

She raised the phone back to her ear and smiled. "Did you come too, Sir?" she asked, quietly.

She heard him laugh softly before replying, "Yes, my love, I did. The sound of you coming like that completely undid me. Knowing you're on a busy commuter bus helped."

She laughed. "I can't believe you just made me do that."

"You deserved your release for obeying me so beautifully. So, what are your plans tonight?"

"Dawn's coming round for dinner and they've invited me to join them. What time's your flight back?"

Adam laughed. "You booked it. You should know."

Oh yeah. They spoke for a few more minutes until the bus arrived at Rachel's stop. As she stepped off onto the pavement, her body felt lighter than it had all day. With a big smile on her face, she set off with a fresh bounce in her step.

* * * *

Later that evening, after a delicious meal of roast chicken with all the trimmings, Rachel sat back and quietly watched Mandy and Dawn's easy-going banter as they cleared the dishes. She envied the equality of their relationship. Even though Mandy was clearly the one in control in the bedroom, they were completely equal outside of it. In fact, Dawn was so forthright and assertive, that anyone would think that it was Dawn who was the Domme and Mandy, the sub.

Mandy had happily fetched more wine from the kitchen when Dawn had asked her, and had insisted on cooking, serving dinner and helping with clearing away afterwards. There was no hierarchy, no one was in control. They were equals as far as they were concerned. Mandy didn't expect Dawn to address her as Mistress when they weren't playing and she certainly didn't decide what Dawn should eat or drink.

That was what she wanted with Adam. But if she were to become his slave, she would never be his equal and that didn't sit well with her.

"How's your back?" asked Dawn, as Mandy left them to make some coffee.

Rachel grimaced and shrugged. "It's okay. A bit sore, but not as much as it was."

Dawn nodded, sympathetically. "That was a particularly nasty whip Dominique used. It not only would have left permanent scars, but it could have killed you. If she'd caught any vital organs, especially the kidneys..." She trailed off, obviously not wanting to voice the obvious danger Rachel had been in.

Rachel shuddered. "Are there really people who get off on that level of pain?"

Dawn nodded slowly. "Yeah, but only when it's consensual and inflicted by someone who knows what they're doing. Even a hard-core masochist wouldn't have coped with what Dominique was planning on doing to you."

"I didn't know she was his ex-wife until she told me. Adam had refused to talk to me about her." Rachel couldn't help the accusing tone that had crept into her voice. Adam was right, if she'd known who she was, she would never have gone with her that night.

"Don't be too hard on Adam," said Dawn, softly. "Luke told me he'd been desperate to do the right thing by offering Karen a way out. She was driving him mad with her wild demands and it got to the point when the mere mention of her name was enough to make him angry. Apparently, his actual words were that he didn't want to tarnish your relationship with her poison."

"It's not that I blame him," sighed Rachel, "and I do understand why he didn't want to tell me, but sometimes I feel…"

"What?" asked Dawn.

Rachel shrugged. "Oh, nothing. I guess I'm just trying to get my head around this whole equality thing. I can't help wondering if he didn't tell me because he didn't think I was worthy of knowing. Not because he doesn't care for me. I know he does. But, maybe he thinks I don't have the right to know too much about his life because he wants me to be his slave."

Dawn laughed. "What the hell are you going on about? Being someone's slave doesn't make you any less worthy than anyone else. I happen to know that Masters value and care deeply for their slaves."

Mandy came back into the room with the coffee and looked questioningly at Dawn. "What's that about slaves?"

"I was just telling Rachel that most Masters treasure their slaves and treat them really well." Dawn flushed slightly as Mandy put the drinks down and gave her a stern look.

"Slaves, eh?" She walked up to Dawn, hands on her hips and glared down at her. "Get on the floor," she growled.

Bloody hell. Where did that come from?

Rachel didn't want to get caught up in some kinky sex scene and was just about to make a hasty exit, when Dawn said, "Get lost." Then she burst into laughter and playfully thumped Mandy's arm.

Mandy turned to Rachel with exaggerated indignation. "See? You just can't get a decent slave these days."

Although Rachel laughed with them, she couldn't help the heavy feeling sitting in the pit of her stomach. She didn't care how much Masters valued their slaves. It still didn't make her want to be one.

* * * *

As she was getting ready for bed, her unease increased when she got a text from Adam.

I'm back from Birmingham now. Remember, I won't take no for an answer. Night night, gorgeous.

She lay awake for a long time trying to get her head around the whole slave thing. One thing was sure — she didn't want to lose Adam. So, that just left one option, but that was the problem. It wasn't the option of her choice. What should she do?

Chapter Three

The following afternoon, Rachel glanced at her watch and frowned. It was nearly five o'clock. She looked over at Adam's closed door and wondered if she would get to see him later. He'd been holed up in his office for most of the day, preparing for tomorrow's board meeting, and she had hardly seen him except for the few times she'd brought him his coffee.

Last night, her insecurities had escaped from the confinement of her subconscious and had crept unnervingly back to taunt her consciousness. This morning, she'd woken up feeling groggy and edgy, and had hoped for a reassuring cuddle with Adam before his first meeting.

But now, it would soon be time to go home and he still hadn't made any attempt to share a private moment with her. Was he avoiding her? Was her hesitation in making the ultimate commitment to him pissing him off so much that he was having second thoughts? She fiddled distractedly with a pen and closed her eyes. This was hardly helping her with her trust issues. She'd barely been able to concentrate on work since the weekend. She kept making stupid little mistakes and had, yet again, made herself look completely incompetent to Lord Granville's PA, the perfect Linda, when she'd sent her the wrong report for tomorrow's meeting. Adam had been unusually patient with her, but knowing him, that patience would start to wear thin very soon.

Her phone rang suddenly, the shrill sound piercing the silence and making her jump. She picked it up with a tinge of annoyance to hear the receptionist's nasal voice announce that a Mr King and a Miss Roberts had arrived for a five o'clock appointment with Mr Stone. *Huh?* She glanced at the diary and frowned. There was no mention of any appointment. Was Adam booking his own meetings now? She told the receptionist to wait a moment and dialed Adam's number.

"Yes?" His voice sounded strained.

"There's a Mr King and Miss Roberts in reception to see you. They say they have an appointment, but there's nothing in the diary." She held her breath as she waited for Adam to shout something about her being too incompetent to keep the diary up to date, but he just sighed and told her to send them up.

She called back down to reception and told them to send the couple up, then turned to her computer so she would look busy when they arrived on the executive floor. She didn't look up when she heard the lift ping, just pretended to be busy reading something very important on her screen, so when she heard a deep, sexy voice say, "Hello, Rachel," she jumped slightly and looked up in surprise to see Luke and Dominique standing in front of her desk.

"Oh. Hi," she said, not quite able to keep the shock out of her voice. What the hell were they doing here? "Er, one minute, I'll let Adam know you're here."

Before she could pick up the phone to announce their arrival though, Adam opened his door and gestured for them to go in. His face was strained, his mouth set in a rigid line, giving away the seriousness of the impending meeting. As they walked past her toward Adam's office, Luke gave her a warm smile, but Dominique—or rather, Karen—glared at her with such vehemence that an involuntary shudder ran through her. What was going on?

The door shut, leaving her alone again and she tried to refocus her mind back to work. She needed to do a final check to make sure everything was ready for tomorrow's board meeting, but her hands were shaking so much when she opened her organizer that she had to give up. Her mind was buzzing with questions, the main one being, why the hell were Luke and Dominique there?

Finally, she stood up in frustration and started pacing the floor near the lift area. It was far enough away from Adam's office that they wouldn't see her restless shadow through the frosted glass partition and it would give her a chance to look as if she were returning from the kitchen if they came out unexpectedly. As she paced, her mind went back to Saturday night and Dominique's fury as she had tied her to the cross. Tears sprang to her eyes as she recalled the feeling of choking on the gag, the panic that had gripped her when she'd realized there was nothing she could do to get help, and the scorching pain as the whip had sliced through the skin on her back.

"Rachel."

She jumped at Adam's voice behind her. She hadn't heard him come out of his office.

"Are you all right?" he said, softly.

She quickly brushed a tear away and turned to him with an attempt at a smile. "Yes. Well, I was just…"

Adam pulled her into his arms and held her tightly. "It's okay, you don't have to explain, I can guess. Come on, Karen has something she wants to say to you."

Rachel stiffened in his arms and pulled away slightly. "No. Adam, I don't want to see her, please don't make me go in there." She knew she was safe with Adam and Luke there, but the thought of coming face to face with *her*, made her feel physically sick.

Adam was insistent. "Come on, it'll be fine, I promise." He took her hand and led her into his office before closing the door firmly behind him.

Luke stood up from his seat on the leather sofa and took Rachel's hand when she approached. "How are you?" he asked softly.

"Okay, thanks," she replied, her voice sounding small.

Luke strode back over to the sofa, pulled Karen up onto her feet and marched her over to where Adam and Rachel were standing.

Luke's warm eyes became cold and his whole demeanor turned hostile and dangerous as he maneuvered Karen so she was facing Rachel head on. His grip on Karen's arm was tight and when he spoke, his voice was low and uncompromising, "Karen. Say what you've got to say to Rachel and then we're leaving."

Karen's downcast eyes rose to meet Rachel's and the two women locked eyes. Rachel was taken aback by the bitter hatred burning in them and knew that the words she was about to hear would not be sincere. "I'm sorry about what I did to you."

No, you're not.

Luke tightened his grip on Karen's arm and growled, "And?"

Karen scowled and spat her words out, "Adam and I are no longer together and he is free to do as he wishes and with whom he wishes."

Well, if they weren't just the most insincere and well-rehearsed words Rachel had ever heard. She had also picked up the unspoken words, dark and threatening, leaving her in no doubt that, as far as Karen was concerned, this was far from over. A chill seeped into Rachel's blood and she looked desperately at Adam and Luke to see if they had noticed the same unspoken threat that she had, but they seemed satisfied with Karen's 'heartfelt' apology.

Luke nodded at Adam and led Karen out by the arm without another word.

Rachel hadn't realized she'd been holding her breath until the door clicked shut and Karen was finally out of the room. Rachel remained standing in the same spot, staring at the door as if the woman was going to come back through any time, and it was only when Adam touched her arm that she tore her gaze away. He led her over to the sofa and gently pushed her down before sitting down next to her.

"She's gone," he said softly, and pulled her into his arms. "And she won't be back."

She snuggled deeper and finally allowed herself to relax a little.

"What's going to happen to her?" she whispered.

"As you know, anyone caught abusing anyone else in the club is banned for life. The fact that she had physically restrained you against your will, took away your ability to call out the club safe word *and* physically assaulted you, is about as serious as it gets."

Adam's voice had trembled with anger as he'd spoken and Rachel felt a shiver run through her and hoped she would never make him that angry.

"The police have been contacted and they'll deal with her now," he continued. "Oh, and she's signed her share of the club back to me."

"What?" Rachel stared at Adam in surprise.

"She didn't really have much choice. There's not much point in owning a club you've been banned from. She finally saw sense and signed." He leaned down and kissed the top of Rachel's head before nodding his head toward some papers lying on the glass coffee table. "It's over, Rachel. She's out of our lives forever, so you don't have to worry about her anymore. Okay?"

Rachel nodded and smiled. She wished she could believe him, but she'd seen the look in Karen's eyes when she'd spoken the words she'd been forced to say. They had held a lethal measure of vengeful hatred and there had been no defeat and certainly no remorse. She shook off the unnerving thought and hugged Adam closer to her, resolving to put the whole Dominique thing out of her mind.

He continued holding her for a few minutes longer until he finally pulled away and visibly switched back to business mode.

"Is everything ready for the board meeting tomorrow?" he asked, his voice sounding controlled and slightly distant.

"Yes, Sir," she replied, suddenly with an urgent need to feel his dominating force. "Everything's ready."

"Good." Then, as if sensing her need for submissive reinforcement, he narrowed his eyes and grabbed her by the hair, forcing her to look up into his eyes. "Who do you belong to, Rachel?"

Ooh, that beautiful, sexy Dom voice again. She melted a little as her heartbeat increased. "You, Sir. Only you."

"Good girl. You will always obey me, Rachel, do you understand?" His voice was a husky growl now and it took all of her strength to draw in the air she needed to reply.

"Yes, Sir." Her voice was husky and when he reached his free hand up to stroke her face, her breath hitched as her eyelids grew heavy.

"What will happen if you don't obey me, Rachel?"

Fuck. She could feel moist heat building between her legs, which were quickly turning to jelly.

"You will punish me, Sir." Her head was spinning now and her body had become so limp from the delirious submission that the only thing keeping her upright was Adam's firm grip on her hair.

"Who am I, Rachel?" The meaning of his words didn't register at first then the penny dropped and she knew exactly what he meant.

"You're my...M...Master, Sir." There, she'd said the M word and right now, God she meant it.

"Yes, Rachel, I'm your Master and don't you forget it."

Oh yes, the somersaults skipped madly around in her tummy. He tightened his hold on her hair, not giving her a chance to look anywhere but at him. He was looking directly into her eyes, his pupils dilating in response to the glossy glaze covering her own.

Yes, this was what she wanted, needed, craved, and Adam knew it.

Through the fog clouding her head, she heard him command her to kneel at his feet and she immediately slid off the sofa and did as he'd said. He pushed her head down onto his lap and held it in place with a firm, strong hand and let her remain there, until a feeling of such deep, beautiful contentment washed over her.

She would happily have remained there for hours, but eventually, too soon, Adam gently lifted her head up toward him and smiled. "That better?" he asked, softly.

"Yes, thank you, Sir." She looked up into his eyes, deeply in awe of his perception of her needs. "How did you know? You know, what I needed...?"

"I've been a Dom for a long time, sweet thing. If I can't tell by now when a sub needs a little mental dominance, then I'll never know." He pulled her up so she was sitting next to him again and ran his hand gently through her hair. "You should go home now."

"Oh, but..." Rachel stared at him in dismay, she wanted to be in his bed, not her own.

But Adam shook his head and said, "I've got work to do here and you'll just distract me. Go home, get some sleep and be here nice and early in the morning." He studied her for a second with a glint in his eye, before adding, "Remember, no bra or panties and make sure you wear a short skirt. That's an order."

"Yes, Sir." She smiled and started to get up from the sofa.

"Oh, and Rachel?"

"Yes, Sir?"

"You called me your Master. I liked that. A lot."

His eyes flashed with triumph and pride and a deep flush burned her face when she remembered her willingness to surrender so completely to him.

"Good night," she whispered, then stood up and left without another word.

* * * *

"He definitely wants me to be his slave." Rachel finished her rum and cola then banged the empty glass down onto the stained, wooden table. The bar was relatively quiet and the people at the next table turned and gave her an odd look. Whether it was the noise of the glass or her stark words they had heard, she couldn't tell.

Mandy spluttered as she tried to hold back her laughter. "What, you? A slave? I thought you were joking last night?"

"It's not funny." Rachel scowled and reached over for the fresh drink she'd just bought. "He's adamant it's what he wants, but it's not what I want. Oh, Mandy, what am I going to do?"

Mandy gave her a hard stare. "Have you told him how you feel?"

Rachel hesitated. Had she? She thought back to each time he'd brought it up and shifted uncomfortably in her seat as she realized that, rather than be straight with him, she had, in fact, avoided answering him. On Sunday when he'd said he would collar her no matter what, she'd been so scared she'd hastily changed the subject and left shortly afterwards.

"I...er, I haven't actually said it in so many words, but..." She looked at her friend with wide eyes. Had she somehow given him the impression that she would be happy to be his slave? She thought back to earlier that afternoon when she'd been in that beautiful, deep submissive state and had actually called him Master. Why had she done that if she was so sure she didn't want a Total Power Exchange relationship?

Mandy took her hand and gave it a squeeze. "Babe, you need to tell him how you feel. It sounds like he's pretty serious about this and if you do want different things out of this, you need to sort it now before things get more serious."

"It already is getting serious," muttered Rachel. She'd been so preoccupied with all her stupid issues from the past and then the whole Dominique thing at the weekend, that she hadn't been straight with Adam. And she was the one with trust issues? Shit, she would have to tell him and he would be really pissed off with her for not being open with him.

"Promise me you'll tell him as soon as you can," said Mandy, firmly. "If you both want different things from your relationship then you'll both end up getting hurt. If you're really sure you don't want to be his twenty-four-seven slave, and he won't accept anything less, then it'll only be a matter of time before it tears you apart."

The pain that seared Rachel's heart was worse than anything she had ever felt before. The idea of losing Adam was too much to bear, she needed him and, yes, she loved him. But should she give in and agree to be his slave just so she wouldn't lose him?

As if reading her mind, Mandy interrupted her thoughts. "Don't you dare agree to this if it's not what you truly want, Rach. Think about it. How long would you last, being told what to eat and wear, and having to ask permission to sleep or even take a piss, for fuck sake? You may be a sexual submissive, but you haven't got a submissive bone in your body when it comes to day to day living. Look at me, Rachel, it would be a disaster."

"Yeah, yeah, I know," snapped Rachel. Mandy was right. A TPE might work for some people, but she knew herself well enough to know that it wasn't for her.

"The way I see it, you got two choices, honey. Agree to the TPE and you'll be totally miserable, or say no and carry on as you are and let Adam be miserable, if he doesn't dump you, that is. Either way, it doesn't bode well for your relationship."

Mandy's words weren't meant to hurt her, she knew that, but that didn't stop the tears welling up in her eyes as she tried to search her heart for the answer. But, no matter how she looked at it, she just couldn't see how she was going to have her happy ever after.

Chapter Four

Rachel stepped out of the lift at precisely eight o'clock the following morning and came face to face with Adam's steely glare.

"You're late," he snapped.

"What? Adam, it's eight o'clock. Two hours before the board meeting starts and an hour earlier than my official start time." She pushed past him and made her way to her desk, knowing he would be following her.

She wasn't too bothered about Adam's snappy mood, in fact, she'd been expecting it. She knew he was stressed about this meeting today. Lord Granville was being a pain in the arse about something and the whole Dominique thing hadn't exactly helped his stress levels.

She put her takeaway coffee on her desk and turned to hand him the one she'd gotten for him. She'd gotten into the habit of stopping at Starbucks each morning to get them both a coffee on her way to work and, if he had time, they would drink it together before they got on with their respective jobs.

"Sorry." He grinned sheepishly and took his coffee. They made their way into his office, shutting the door on their way. Nobody dared disturb Adam Stone when his door was shut, even if Rachel wasn't at her desk to shield him from any visitors.

Sitting next to each other on the sofa, they ran through the agenda, double-checking all the paperwork was in order and, once Adam was happy that all was well, he put his coffee down and pulled her close. Hmm, he smelled freshly showered, the slight musky scent of his deodorant teasing her nostrils. Her pulse quickened as the scent reminded her of their shower last week and she glanced wistfully over at the bathroom door, wishing they could do it all again now.

Adam ran his finger lightly over the soft material covering her breasts and grinned as her nipple instantly hardened under his touch. He then reached down to her legs and stroked her thigh, before sliding his hand under the short skirt she'd worn, as ordered. When his fingers reached her bare pussy and gently probed her entrance, she groaned.

"Good girl for obeying my orders," he growled.

She felt herself moisten at his words and a deep sense of well-being enveloped her.

"Get up and follow me," he said suddenly, and pulled her up to stand. Silently, and without question, she followed him into the boardroom. "I want you to serve the coffee yourself once everyone is seated."

She frowned in surprise. "But, I thought everyone just helps themselves?"

Adam swatted her ass, just hard enough to sting. "Today, *you* serve them. Understood?"

"Yes, Sir," she mumbled, annoyed at having to play waitress for them. She wondered why he suddenly demanded that she serve them when, only yesterday, he'd told her to just leave the coffee on the table.

"Bend over the table," he said.

She giggled, not sure she'd heard right. In about an hour and a half's time, the whole Board of Directors would be sitting around this table and he wanted to fuck her there now?

"I won't say it again, Rachel."

Oh shit, he's bloody serious. Without another word she turned toward the table and slowly lowered her upper body onto the cool, polished wood. He pushed her legs so her body was completely flush with the table, giving her no room to move, and she sighed as he started stroking the soft skin of her arse.

"I want to mark your lovely ass," he said, his voice suddenly gruff and raw. "But not now. Today we try something new."

She remained silent and wondered what on earth he was going to do this time. She soon found out as something cold and wet spread over the opening to her arse followed immediately by something hard pressing against her tight hole.

"No," she cried, and tried to stand up in panic.

"Sssh." Adam pushed her back down and held her in place with a firm hand on her back. "This won't hurt, I promise. It's a small butt plug, the smallest there is. Please try it for me and if you really hate it, I won't ask you again."

A nervous shudder ran through her as she replied, "Okay." She wanted to please him and if this pleased him, then she would do it.

"Good girl. Relax your muscles and it'll slip in easily." His voice, although still holding an excited edge, comforted her and she allowed herself to relax as the hand on her back started gently massaging between her shoulder blades.

She stiffened as the alien object probed a little farther, but relaxed again when Adam stopped and continued his massage. Then there was a deep burning sensation and she moaned a little, more from discomfort than actual pain. The burning got worse though and she was just about to cry out for him to stop when it slipped in with a little plop and the burning went away.

She waited for the pain, but all she felt was full and, oddly enough, aroused. Adam wriggled the plug slightly, sending little shivers through her and she whimpered as nerve endings she hadn't known existed, sparked excitedly to life. He rubbed his finger along her slit and when he pushed it through her folds, she was shocked at how easily it slid into her soaking wet pussy.

"Oh, Rachel," he whispered, and pushed his solid erection against her arse. He teased her clit and the combination of the new sensations from the plug and his coarse fingers rubbing her throbbing nub, was all it took to take her to a new level of pleasure. Just as the first telltale signs of orgasm started building though, he removed his hand, causing Rachel to emit a groan of frustration.

"Please, Adam. Please let me come." She needed to come and she needed it now, but Adam moved away from her and slapped her arse.

"Get up," he said, firmly. "If you behave, I promise you'll get your orgasm later."

Rachel pulled herself up from the table, squirming at the unfamiliar fullness in her arse as she straightened her body. She frowned as it dawned on her what he was up to. He was going to make her serve the coffee in the meeting, fully aroused and with a fucking butt plug shoved up her arse. If she performed to his liking, he would reward her with an orgasm after the meeting and if she didn't...

She put her hands on her hips and glared at him. "Adam, I know how seriously you take this business and these meetings. Do you seriously want to risk your reputation if anyone guesses what you're up to?"

Adam just laughed though. "My dear Rachel, what makes you think it'll be my reputation on the line? As far as they would be concerned, you're just an over-amorous temp who's behaving like a whore in my boardroom."

Even though Adam's crude words were so harsh, Rachel's knees went weak as heat shot through her body. He was right—he would just look shocked and outraged and she would be the one having to live with the shame. He knew she wouldn't risk that, and he clearly also knew that the whole idea of the risk of being caught behaving like a whore turned her on in a way she would never have known herself.

"Adam Stone, you are one sick bastard." She scowled, as her body quivered again with arousal.

He laughed as he slid his hand up her skirt and brushed against her burning pussy. He held up his finger, glistening with her juices, and raised his eyebrows. "Who, me?"

Despite this slightly scary turn in their erotic play, Rachel couldn't hold back the naughty grin she'd been trying to hide. Damn him, but this was so sexy.

"I'll serve your coffee, Sir, and will behave with the utmost decorum." She lifted her chin and walked out of the boardroom and into his office. The plug moved as she did and the sensation was nearly enough to send her over the edge right there and then. Maybe a quick trip to the bathroom would help to ease the tension so she didn't spill any coffee.

"Oh, and Rachel?"

"Yes, Sir?" She could hear the quiver in her voice as she turned awkwardly back to face him.

"You don't have permission to pleasure yourself. Do I make myself clear?"

God, she'd like to wipe that smirk of his face.

"Yes, *Sir*," she hissed, and walked as gracefully out of his office as she could, all things considered.

About an hour later, people had started arriving for the meeting. Lord Granville was already there, along with a couple of other directors. Just before the meeting was due to start, Joanne Baker, the Finance Director, rushed past her desk. She stopped briefly when she saw Rachel, and smiled. "Can we have a chat after the meeting? I've got a proposition for you."

"Oh. Yes, of course," said Rachel, wondering what on earth Joanne Baker could possibly want with her.

When the final person had arrived, Adam popped his head round the door. "Can you bring in the lunch at twelve-thirty please?"

"Yes, Mr Stone," Rachel purred, sounding every bit the professional she intended to be.

"Oh, and you can serve the coffee now." He paused in the doorway while she rose from her chair, and grinned when she squirmed as the plug moved in her arse.

Once in the privacy of the kitchen, Rachel let out the nervous breath she'd been holding. She was so aroused, she barely knew what day it was, but she'd be damned if she would make it obvious for him. After all, he was making her suffer by withholding her much-needed orgasm. Well, two could play at that game! She would be as cool as a cucumber when she served that coffee. No one would guess a thing and he'd owe her big time.

She grinned to herself as she carried the coffee jug toward the boardroom. She knocked and walked in. *Game on, Adam Stone.*

"Ah, Miss Porter, come in. My very efficient PA is going to serve the coffee now," he said smoothly.

He grinned at her as she walked as gracefully as she could, heading deliberately to the opposite end of the table so she would serve him last.

As she leaned over Lord Granville to pour the coffee into his porcelain cup, her breasts, without their usual support, fell forwards. She knew her nipples would be hard so anyone looking at her now would easily work out she wasn't wearing a bra. Thankfully, they were all focused on what Joanne Baker was saying and she got past the first couple of people with no problems.

She moved smoothly, trying not to look too obvious as the plug teased her nerve endings. "Are you all right, Miss Porter?" Adam's voice snapped her back to attention. "You seem to be walking a little awkwardly."

Bastard! "Yes, thank you, Mr Stone. I twisted my ankle earlier, that's all." *Ha, that'll shut you up.*

She continued serving the coffee, aware of his eyes on her the whole time. A quick glance around the table told her no one else was paying attention and she relaxed slightly and allowed herself to flash him a little smile. He'd known no one would notice her, she realized. He'd just wanted to wind her up.

Finally everyone had their coffee except for Adam, who was sitting at the head of the table. As she leaned over his shoulder to pour his coffee, his hand crept slowly up the back of her thigh until it reached her arse. She looked around and was thankful that, from where he was sitting, it would be difficult for anyone to see where his hand had gone. Her legs weakened slightly as her body thought it might finally get its reward, and it took all of her willpower to force herself to look cool, calm and collected.

Then the bastard pulled slightly on the plug and jiggled it a little bit. She couldn't help it—she let out a gasp of shock as the sensation increased the intense ripples of pleasure pulsing through her body. Everyone looked up and she quickly feigned a little sneeze. "Excuse me." She smiled and straightened back up when she'd finished pouring Adam's coffee.

"Bless you," said Joanne, barely looking up from her papers.

"Thank you." Adam moved his hand slowly down her leg again and she was finally able to make her exit, with her modesty and reputation intact.

Once outside the boardroom, she leaned back against the door and allowed herself to breathe normally again. Fuck, he'd really pushed his luck.

She made her way back to her desk and slowly lowered herself onto her chair, careful not to put too much pressure on the plug. She was surprised that it didn't actually hurt and even more surprised that it was as sexy as it was. As long as Adam didn't get any ideas about anything too big, she supposed she wouldn't mind doing it again.

"Miss Porter, a word please."

She hadn't heard Adam come out of the boardroom and jumped slightly as she looked up at him. He nodded toward the kitchen and she quickly got up and followed him. As soon as the door had closed behind them, he gathered her in his arms and nuzzled her neck.

"Thank you for making such a dull meeting so much fun," he said, nibbling her ear gently. "You have no idea how much I hate these meetings."

"You're very welcome, Sir," said Rachel, surprised at his revelation. She'd never have thought Adam Stone hated this necessary side to the business.

He pushed her against the wall and pinned her arms to her sides. "Now, I believe I owe you an orgasm," he murmured, and slowly brought his hand up her skirt until it reached its target. He moved his hand slowly back and pulled on the plug, dislodging it to the point she thought he was removing it, but then he pushed it back in again and fresh sensations rippled through her body.

"Ohhh," she groaned and closed her eyes.

"Touch your breasts," he ordered. "Pull and squeeze your nipples. Hard." As he said it, he found her entrance and he moaned as he slid a finger deep inside her.

Rachel reached under her blouse and soon became lost in the sensations taking over her body — her nipples burning from being pinched by her fingers, Adam's fingers inside her pussy while he played with the plug with his other hand. As the waves started building, Adam suddenly pulled the plug out and her knees buckled slightly as the sudden emptiness overwhelmed her. She just about managed to slap her hand over her mouth to stop herself from crying out loud, as her control shattered and her body finally received its delicious reward.

As she slowly recovered, Adam pulled her half-slumped body back up into his arms and held her tight. "God, you're amazing," he breathed, and planted lots of light kisses on her head.

All too soon though, he pulled away and sighed regrettably. "I'd better get back in there," he groaned. "I told them I had an urgent call to make. See you later."

"Adam?"

He stopped in the doorway and turned around, "Yes?" he said, softly.

"Thank you." She knew he'd know what she meant. It wasn't just the orgasm she was thanking him for, but the fact that he'd pushed her boundaries, making her feel terrified of being caught, but all along knowing she'd be all right. She knew without a doubt that if anyone in that boardroom had looked up and seen anything untoward, he'd have covered for her.

He gave her a wink and left, leaving her body still shuddering slightly with the aftershocks of her powerful release.

The next hour and a half passed in a daze. Something was niggling at her though and she couldn't work out what it was. It was as if her subconscious seemed to want to tell her something, but it couldn't quite reach her conscious mind through the dreamy cloud of euphoria floating in her head. It was only when Adam came out of the boardroom and asked her to bring in the platters of sandwiches, that she realized what she'd forgotten and the bottom dropped out of her stomach as she stared at him in shock.

"The...the food hasn't arrived yet," she said, her voice only just audible. Oh, God, why hadn't she noticed the catering company hadn't yet delivered the food? She should have checked and chased it up at least an hour ago. She felt her face pale as Adam glared at her in disbelief. "Hang on," she said, with false confidence, "they're probably waiting in reception."

Her fingers trembled as she dialed reception to ask if they'd been delivered and her heart sank further when the indifferent receptionist told her that no one had delivered anything. She put the phone down and looked up at Adam in despair.

His eyes flashed with anger as he realized her mistake, the deep blue turning icy cold and hard. "Sort it, *now*," he growled, and stormed back into the meeting.

Oh shit, shit, shit, what's happened? She was sure she had placed the order on the catering company's website—she remembered doing it. She grabbed the phone and quickly dialed their number, praying they would apologize and say that they were on their way.

"I'm sorry, Miss Porter, we don't seem to have received any order from your company." The girl sounded apologetic and double-checked the system to make sure there hadn't been a mistake, but she only confirmed that they had definitely not received an order.

Rachel closed her eyes, desperately clutching at straws as she asked, "Is there any way you could…"

"I'm sorry, there's no way we could arrange anything at this short notice. Sorry."

Not as sorry as I'm going to be, Rachel thought, desperately. She quickly logged onto their website and signed in. Tears stung her eyes as she stared at the unconfirmed order on the screen in front of her. She had a vague memory of wanting to check how many vegetarians were attending and had obviously forgotten to go back and confirm the order.

She glanced at the door to Adam's office and her stomach knotted up into a tight ball of fear. This was a major fuck-up and it was all her fault.

Adam was going to kill her.

Chapter Five

"If Mr Stone asks where I am, tell him I've gone to get their lunch," Rachel called to the bewildered looking receptionist, and rushed out of the rotating doors leading to the street. She ran across the road to the little deli where she usually bought her sandwiches.

"Hello, Rachel," said the owner, Mario, with a warm smile, "would you like your usual?"

She gasped as she tried to get her words out and had to take a couple of deeps breaths before she could speak. "Actually, Mario, you might just be able to save my life."

Ten minutes later, Rachel was riding back up to her office in the lift, her arms laden with bags of pre-packaged sandwiches, fruit and silver foil platters. Although pre-packaged for convenience, the sandwiches were always freshly made on the premises every morning and the fillings were always generous and tasty.

She ran into the small kitchen and hurriedly ripped open the packaging then placed the sandwiches on the platters. Mario had given her some lettuce and cherry tomatoes for decoration and lent her a glass bowl for the fruit as there wasn't enough time to prepare and chop it — it would have to do.

Only twenty minutes after she should have originally brought in their lunch, she knocked briefly on the door to the boardroom and walked confidently in, carrying the platters of sandwiches. "Sorry for the delay," she said, as if in full control. "The caterers were held up in traffic."

She glanced over at Adam who shot her an odd look, then hurried out again to make some fresh coffee. It was only after they'd finished their lunch and had resumed the agenda that Rachel finally allowed herself to sit back and take stock of the situation. *Phew, that was close, too close.* Adam had looked really cross. Even though she'd managed to save the day, she knew he wouldn't let her off lightly.

The door clicked and Rachel looked up to see Joanne Baker coming toward her. "Just nipping to the ladies," she said, smiling. "Great lunch, by the way, better than usual."

"Oh, thanks." Rachel's face flamed, but she couldn't bring herself to admit her mistake to Joanne.

"Oh, it looks like things are going to drag on a bit." Joanne rolled her eyes. "Lord Granville is being particularly pedantic today. Can we have our chat tomorrow instead?"

"Yes, of course," said Rachel, forcing a bright smile onto her face. *If I haven't been fired,* she thought, bitterly.

Joanne had been right. The meeting dragged well into the afternoon and, by the time everyone had gone, it was after three o'clock. She wanted to go in and see Adam, to apologize for her mistake and, hopefully, hear him thank her for fixing things.

Before she had a chance though, Adam stormed out of his office. "I'm going out," he snapped as he passed her desk without looking at her. "I don't know when I'll be back."

"Okay," she said quietly, feeling her heart sink at his tone. *God, he must be really angry.*

"Oh, and can you book me onto the earliest flight to Amsterdam out of Heathrow tomorrow." His voice was brusque, unforgiving.

"Amsterdam? Er, yes, Sir. When will you be returning?" She'd known he was due to meet with some important clients from Amsterdam soon, but she'd understood it was going to be a video conference from his office. Was he so angry with her that he would rather travel abroad for the day than face her in the office?

"I don't know," he snapped. "Leave the return open. See you later."

He strode away from her desk and stepped into the lift without looking back. As the doors closed, she felt a lump in her throat and quickly picked up the phone to call the company travel agent before she forgot and dug herself deeper into the shit she was already in.

* * * *

Rachel was reeling. After yesterday's debacle, could things really get any weirder? As Joanne Baker walked away, Rachel could only stare after her in shock, her heart thumping with excitement. Was Joanne serious?

After a restless night dreaming about boardrooms and fucked-up lunches, Rachel had gone into work this morning feeling listless and grumpy. The fact that she wouldn't see Adam all day was both a relief and a disappointment. Was Adam still pissed off with her? Surely not, but wouldn't he have called her if everything were okay?

She'd been deep in her thoughts and hadn't noticed the elegant Finance Director hovering at her desk, until she had spoken. "Rachel?"

She had jumped and immediately slapped her professional, Miss Super Efficient PA face on. "Hi, Joanne," she'd said, smiling.

"Got time for that chat now?" Without waiting for an answer, Joanne had turned and walked into Adam's office, sat down on the sofa and waited, expectantly.

Rachel had followed her in, feeling odd for using Adam's office without him there. *I miss him. Oh for God's sake,* she'd scolded herself silently, *he's only gone for a day. Pull yourself together.*

Joanne had then studied her for a moment before she'd spoken. "Has Adam said anything about when the new girl starts? You know, Lucy's maternity cover?"

New girl? Rachel had been so absorbed in her new job that she kept forgetting it wasn't permanent. How funny that she'd been so terrified of working for Adam when she'd first found out about her temporary promotion. He was scary, yes, but in a completely different way from anything she could ever have imagined. The truth was, she was enjoying herself now and the sudden reminder that it would all end sometime soon, had brought her back down to earth with a great big bump.

Actually, he was probably still so pissed off with her for screwing up the lunch order yesterday that he would fire her anyway. What would happen if he did fire her, would he still want her as his sub?

"Rachel?" Joanne's voice had brought her back out of her gloomy thoughts and she'd returned her attention to the lady sitting opposite her.

"Sorry." She'd smiled, with an outward appearance of calm. "Lucy's replacement? To be honest, he hasn't mentioned it. Why?"

Joanne had leaned forwards and lowered her voice, as if drawing her into a conspiracy. "Well, after you looked over those figures for me a couple of weeks ago, I checked your personnel records because I was so impressed with what you did."

Oh, Rachel had forgotten all about that.

Joanne continued, her voice low. "Those mistakes that you spotted were very complex and had been missed by our accountants. When you picked up on them straight away, I knew you had to have some sort of talent with numbers. I was surprised to see that you didn't go to university though?"

It was a question, not a statement, and Rachel knew Joanne was waiting for an explanation. "It was a difficult time," she'd said, quietly, not wanting to go into detail. "My parents both died around the time I was considering what to do and I never got around to doing anything more about it."

Joanne had looked genuinely sad and her words had sounded sincere when she'd said, "Oh, Rachel, that's awful, I'm so sorry."

Rachel had shrugged and looked away to hide the painful memories from her face. "That's okay, it was a long time ago."

"Come and work for me," Joanne had blurted suddenly, her face lighting back up.

"What?" Rachel had gawped at Joanne as if she'd just proposed marriage.

"I need someone like you on my team," she'd said, not bothering to hide her enthusiasm. "You've got a keen eye for detail and are very talented with numbers. You'd make a great accountant."

"But…" Rachel had started to protest but, actually, she knew Joanne was right so there was no point acting all modest and coy.

"No buts," said Joanne. Her voice had taken on an edge that showed how determined she was about this, and Rachel was flattered that she was effectively being headhunted by this powerful lady. "We'll send you to college part-time to get your accounting qualifications and you'll get all the practical training you need here."

"Well, I…"

"Good. That's settled then."

They had then both stood up and shaken hands, sealing the agreement.

"What about Adam?" He was going to be pretty pissed off when he found out she had been stolen from under his nose. Or maybe he'd be glad? It would save him having to fire her.

Joanne had just smiled, that confident professional smile that said she wasn't going to let such a minor detail get in her way. "Leave Adam to me," she'd said. "If we assure him you'll stay until Lucy's replacement starts, he can't really argue, can he?"

And with that, Joanne had walked out, leaving Rachel staring after her in disbelief. Wow, she'd just been offered a new job. The blood buzzed through her veins as excitement replaced her surprise. She'd always wanted to work with numbers, she knew she was good, and the idea of working with something she was good at, gave her such a feeling of confidence that she wanted to jump up and down like an excited child.

What would Adam say? He'd probably be pleased to be rid of her—after all, if he had to go to the extreme of flying off to Amsterdam for the day just to avoid her, then she'd be doing him a favor.

At four o'clock, her phone rang. "Adam Stone's office, can I help you?" She had settled so comfortably into her role as Adam's PA that anyone on the other end of the phone would assume she was his long-standing assistant.

"Hi." Adam's voice sounded strained, distant.

"Hi," she answered, suddenly not sure what to say to him. "How's the trip?" Duh, couldn't she have thought of something a little more original to say?

"Okay. Is everything all right at the office? Any messages?" He still sounded distant.

Her heart sank at the cool, impersonal tone of his voice.

She ran through a couple of things with him, relayed a few messages and assured him that everything was fine. *Oh, and I've been offered another job, so fuck you,* she thought silently.

Once business had been dealt with, he ended the call with a brisk, "See you tomorrow."

She put the receiver down and stared at it for a few minutes. God, he was still angry with her.

Suddenly, a flash of anger tore through her and she threw her pen down onto the desk. "Fuck you, Adam Stone," she hissed aloud.

Okay, she'd screwed up the lunch order, but her quick thinking had saved the day and no one had been any the wiser. Except for him. Surely he should be commending her for acting so calmly and quickly? The more she thought about it, the more it didn't make sense. Her small mistake didn't justify his aloof and angry manner, so there had to be more to it and there was only one other reason for it that she could think of. He was getting tired of her. Maybe he realized she didn't want a TPE relationship and didn't feel she was worth bothering with. He probably thought her mistake yesterday would be a good excuse to distance himself from her.

But, on the other hand, he had seemed so happy when she'd called him Master, and yesterday, when he'd rewarded her in the kitchen, he had been anything but distant. It didn't make sense. What was going on?

She continued to torment herself until it was time to go home, by which time she had convinced herself that Adam was definitely going to dump her as soon as he got back from his trip, and find himself a nice, willing slave to serve him.

The following morning, she fidgeted nervously with his coffee as she steeled herself to go into his office. The door was open, but he didn't call out to her as he usually did. *Uh-oh, not a good sign.*

She popped her head round the door and stuck a smile on her face. "Good morning," she said, briskly, and walked toward his desk.

He was bent over some report or other, seemingly engrossed, and ignored her greeting. As she placed the cup down on a coaster in front of him, he finally looked up and gave her a smile of sorts. "Oh, hello. Thanks."

She was shocked at how tired he looked. His eyes were slightly hollowed and dark shadows beneath them made him look almost haunted. Previously unnoticeable lines were now etched across his brow, which seemed to have frozen in a permanent frown.

But it was the fact that he hadn't shaved that shocked Rachel the most. At work, Adam was always well-groomed, his suit crisp and sharp, his face closely shaven and his hair neat and stylish.

Today, though, he looked like he'd just stumbled in after a rough night at Boundaries, his hair unkempt and his suit rumpled.

"Are you okay?" she cried, not able to keep the shock out of her voice.

He nodded and ran his hand though his hair. "Yes, I'm just tired, that's all."

When she didn't give any sign of letting him get away with such a vague answer, he added, "I came straight here from the airport last night and have been working all night. I didn't realize it was this late."

She wanted to walk around the desk and massage his shoulders for him, he looked so tense and exhausted, but the fear that he was still angry stopped her. Instead she remained where she was, and wondered what to say next.

"I've left some reports on your desk. I'm not to be disturbed by anyone, except Lord Granville."

And with that she knew she was dismissed.

She struggled through the morning, shielding calls and visitors and worrying about what was wrong. Adam remained in his office the whole time and barely acknowledged her when she brought him some coffee at eleven o'clock.

Finally, at half-past twelve, his door opened and he emerged looking, if possible, even worse than before. "I'm going home to get some sleep," he said, his voice sounding croaky with exhaustion. "My car will pick you up at eight o'clock sharp, make sure you're ready. Oh, and bring a weekend bag."

Before she had a chance to comprehend his words, Adam was gone. *Car? Weekend bag?* She'd been so sure he'd been about to either fire her or dump her, or both, she was stunned by what he'd just said. That meant he wanted to see her tonight. And he wanted her to stay for the whole weekend. Why?

Maybe he was building up to one final ultimatum? Or maybe he was so sure she'd willingly become his slave that he planned to keep her chained and naked all weekend. Or maybe he really was going to dump her and he just wanted to use her one last time then throw her out like an unwanted toy?

* * * *

Later that evening, when she was ready and packed, she poured Mandy and herself a large glass of wine each.

"Has it occurred to you that he might just want to spend the weekend with you with no ulterior motives?" Mandy rolled her eyes at Rachel and took the glass. "Honestly, give the guy a break. You don't know what the problem is. It could just be something related to work."

"So how come he turned all funny on me the moment he realized I'd fucked up the lunch order?" Rachel pouted, knowing that she sounded like a petulant teenager, but she just couldn't help herself.

Mandy frowned and actually slapped her hard across her bottom.

"Ow," shrieked Rachel, "what did you do that for?"

"Because someone needs to knock some sense into you. You need a good spanking and if it wasn't for the fact that you're off to see Adam later, I'd do it myself."

The anger in Mandy's voice shocked Rachel. *Shit, she's serious.*

Mandy faced Rachel head on, arms akimbo and said, "Don't go jumping to conclusions, Rachel, you don't know what's going on. If you're not careful you're going to push Adam away. You've got to learn to trust him."

"I do trust him," said Rachel, not quite able to keep the sulky tone out of her voice.

"Oh really? So why have you already decided that he's going to use you and dump you? I've only met him the once, but he seems like a decent man to me. Talk to him, find out what it is he wants from you. If he does want to carry on seeing you and wants a TPE relationship, then tell him how you feel about it and take it from there. You must be honest with him though, trust works two ways, you know."

Rachel sighed and took a sip of her wine. Mandy was right, of course. She owed it to Adam to be straight with him. She loved him, more than she'd loved anyone before, even Paul, but no matter how much she loved him and needed him, she wasn't prepared to sacrifice her freedom for him. Not because she didn't think he deserved it, on the contrary, it was because she loved him so much that she didn't want that love to turn to resentment and bitterness when she couldn't live up to his expectations. She understood how a TPE relationship could be a beautiful and precious thing, but she also knew herself well enough to know that she could never live like that.

"Okay," she said, after another sip of wine. "If Adam doesn't finish with me tonight, I'll ask him straight out what he wants and then I'll tell him how I feel about it."

"Good girl," said Mandy, looking pleased.

"God, you're such a natural bloody Domme. You just called me a good girl."

Both girls laughed and the tension lifted again.

"Talking of being open and honest, I've got something I need to tell you," said Mandy, suddenly sounding nervous.

"Oh, no, don't tell me you've switched to being a sub," giggled Rachel.

"As if. Dawn's been offered a job at the New York Times." Mandy eyed Rachel steadily, as if expecting some sort of reaction.

"That's great." She smiled, but then it dawned on her what the implications were and her smile faded. "Oh, does that mean she'll be moving back to New York?"

Mandy nodded. "She's asked me to go back with her."

Rachel put her glass down and put her arms around her friend and gave her a long hug. "Oh, Mandy, I'm really happy for you."

Mandy blinked. "You don't mind?"

"Why would I mind?" laughed Rachel.

"Well, it would mean giving you notice on the flat. It would be a permanent move." Mandy looked so guilty that Rachel almost made her suffer to get her back for smacking her bottom before. But she was genuinely happy for Mandy and couldn't keep the smile off her face.

"Don't worry about the flat. I can probably manage the rent on my own now." She grinned when Mandy looked surprised. "I haven't told you because this is the first time I've seen you since yesterday, but I've been offered a new job and even though I'll be a trainee, I'll still be getting a raise."

"Oh, my God, why the hell didn't you tell me sooner? That's fantastic. Congratulations! Right, you've got twenty minutes before Adam's car picks you up. Spill, and don't leave anything out."

Rachel filled her friend in on all the details of her job offer, losing track of time until the sound of a car horn alerted her to the fact that Rob was waiting outside. She gave Mandy a quick peck on the cheek and grabbed her overnight bag. "See you on Sunday," she called, just before she rushed to the door.

"Yeah, providing you're not enslaved in some dark dungeon at the mercy of your Master," said Mandy, with an evil grin.

As Rachel greeted Rob and climbed into the car, there was a nervous flutter in her belly. Even though she knew Mandy had been joking, a little part of her couldn't help wondering just how determined Adam was to make her his slave.

Chapter Six

Adam was waiting for her when she arrived in the reception at Boundaries. He looked a lot better than he had earlier, the shadows were gone from under his eyes and the deep lines on his brow had relaxed back to barely visible character lines.

"Hello, gorgeous," he said and pulled her into his arms.

"Are you okay?" Rachel asked tentatively. She didn't want to risk upsetting him, but she couldn't forget the troubled man she'd seen at the office earlier.

"I'm fine," he replied softly.

"But..."

He put a finger on her lips. "Sssh," he said. "We'll talk later. Right now I want you naked and on your knees."

"Naked?" Rachel gasped. *Holy shit!*

"Oh all right, I'll settle for you removing your coat for now." He grinned and helped her slip her coat off.

Once he'd handed her coat and bag in at reception, he fastened the leather collar around her neck before putting the wrist and ankle cuffs on her. He stepped back and studied her. Heat stained her cheeks and pooled in her groin as he inspected his property. He nodded with satisfaction, clipped the leash to her collar then led her into the club.

She was wearing a very short, black pencil skirt and a thin, white silk blouse with the top four buttons undone, exposing her braless cleavage. Adam had sent her a text earlier instructing her to wear this outfit, which he had left in a package under his desk. When she'd changed into it and had looked at herself in the mirror, she'd seen a slutty looking secretary staring back at her and a shiver had run through her at the obvious implications.

They made their way through the crowds and she grinned when Chrissie waved to her from the bar. She felt like she'd come home.

As they sat down at their usual table, Amelia came across with a couple of drinks for them. Her friend looked stunning in a purple satin boned corset and not much else. Her light blonde hair was perfectly spiked and her makeup made her blue eyes sparkle. Or was the sparkle because she was happy? She certainly looked radiant.

"Do you work here?" asked Rachel, surprised.

Amelia grinned and shook her head. "Nah. Jack's late so I thought I'd help Chrissie out. I hate sitting around on my own, pretending not to notice the Doms eyeing me up."

Adam laughed and gestured for her to join them. "Well, maybe you two could keep each other company for half an hour or so, then?" He nodded over at one of the Dungeon Monitors. "We've got a new guy starting tonight and I'd like to show him around myself."

Amelia smiled broadly and sat down on the sofa next to Rachel. "Thanks. That would be great."

Adam pulled the ring on Rachel's collar and drew her up close. "Now that Karen is gone, you can move freely around the club."

"Thank you, Sir."

He kissed her hard, holding her firmly in place while he forced her to remember his control over her. When he finally released her, she was panting, her lips were swollen and face flushed. He didn't look that dissimilar.

"I never thought I'd see Adam Stone so smitten," whispered Amelia, as Adam strode away from their table.

"Hmm. He's pretty pissed off with me right now, actually," replied Rachel, taking a sip of her drink to try and recover from the kiss.

Amelia laughed and raised her eyebrows. "Now what have you done?"

Rachel groaned. "I fucked up at work, big time, and to make matters worse, we have differing opinions on where our relationship is heading. I daren't say any more than that or he'll go mad, but let's just say that things are a little tense right now."

"Well, girl, in that case, you need to let you hair down. Come on, they're playing Depeche Mode." Amelia jumped up and grabbed Rachel's hand as the pulsing beat of Personal Jesus filled the club. She dragged Rachel onto the packed dance floor and raised her arms as she swung her hips seductively to the sexy rhythm.

Rachel soon lost herself in the music as she and Amelia danced to the heavy gothic sounds. They flirted subtly with each other, their brief encounter still fresh in Rachel's memory, and their scantily clad bodies soon glistened from the heat surrounding them. The dry ice machine threw occasional plumes of smoke across the dance floor, briefly enveloping them as they danced. It felt good.

Gradually though, the music changed from gothic rock to heavy industrial, and Amelia signaled to Rachel that she'd had enough. After grabbing a couple of bottles of water from the bar, they headed arm in arm across to the far end of the enormous room and found a couple of free seats in a quiet corner.

"What time will Jack get here?" asked Rachel then took a grateful gulp of the ice cold water.

Amelia shrugged. "Dunno. He got held up in a meeting at work. Shouldn't be too long though."

"You're very different when he's not around." Rachel still found it incredible that this confident, outgoing woman became so subservient as soon as Jack was with her. She wondered if her happy sparkle was because he wasn't there.

"This is how I am at work. But I love letting it all go as soon as we get home." She took a swig of the water then continued, "He makes me strip as soon as we walk in through the front door and I have to crawl on my hands and knees unless he gives me permission to walk. It's a complete TPE, and I love it."

Rachel couldn't help gawping at Amelia in surprise. "You're his slave?"

Amelia laughed. "Yeah. Couldn't you tell?"

"I assumed you just played here and went back to normal when you got home."

"Hell no. The only time we're equals is at work and then I outrank him. Otherwise, we live the lifestyle twenty-four-seven." She must have noticed Rachel's look of shock because she then added, "And I wouldn't have it any other way."

"Wow. I didn't realize." So people really could exist happily in a Total Power Exchange. But no matter how happy Amelia obviously was, Rachel didn't envy her.

"I crave his Domination like a druggie craves his next fix," continued Amelia. "I need it. I can't explain it, but it's such an integral part of our lives that to live without it is unthinkable."

"I think that's beautiful," sighed Rachel. "I find the depth of your submission to Jack fascinating. But a bit scary as well. I'm not sure it would be for me."

"I thought that at first as well. But as our relationship grew, so did my need for his dominance." Amelia made it all sound so normal.

"And now you're his slave. You know, you're the last person I would have thought of as being a slave." Rachel shook her head, still not quite able to believe it.

Amelia laughed. "I must admit, before I met Jack, if anyone had told me they wanted me to be his slave, I'd have punched his lights out. Especially after..." She stopped suddenly.

"After what?"

Amelia's eyes clouded over as she stared absently at a couple nearby. The female Domme was tenderly stroking her male sub's head as he knelt by her feet. He had a look of complete devotion on his face and only had eyes for his Mistress.

"Before I got together with Jack, I was in an abusive vanilla relationship for two years. Colin was the complete opposite of Jack — sweet on the outside but a hard, vicious bully on the inside." Amelia lowered her voice as she spoke, as if she didn't want to taint the positive atmosphere of the club. "He made me feel worthless and completely destroyed any confidence I'd had before we'd got together."

"Oh, Amelia, that's awful." Rachel took Amelia's hand and squeezed it. It was hard to imagine this wonderful, vibrant woman being made to feel so bad about herself.

Amelia shrugged and smiled. "Jack is the opposite. He looks rough and tough on the outside, but he's the most caring and supportive person I've ever met in my life. He makes me feel like I'm the most special woman on the planet. He values me and treats me with complete respect, even when I'm on the floor, screaming as he beats me with a crop." She chuckled. "Funny, eh?"

Rachel shook her head. She understood completely and now knew exactly where the sparkle had come from. "I think it's wonderful that you've got such a special relationship."

Amelia smiled. "Yeah, he's pretty cool. Talk of the devil."

Rachel looked up to find Adam and Jack approaching them. She looked at Jack with a newfound respect. Suddenly he didn't seem so scary anymore. Amelia slid off the chair and knelt on the floor ready to greet her Master, and his hard features softened ever so slightly as he towered over his willing slave.

She looked up at Adam and smiled. Would she ever be able to surrender to him so completely? She really wished she could, because then she would truly make him happy.

"Sorry I was so long," he said, softly. Had she just imagined it, or had his own stern features softened slightly as he'd spoken?

"That's okay. Amelia and I were dancing for a while."

He grinned. "I know, I was watching. You're very sexy together." He looked up at Jack and winked. "Maybe we should arrange another scene with the two of them soon?"

Jack laughed and ruffled Amelia's hair. "You're on."

"Come on, sweet thing. I've got plans for you tonight." He took Rachel's hand and pulled her up to stand by him.

Her legs wobbled slightly, but it wasn't from sitting too long. Adam's words had somehow managed to ingrain themselves into the part of her brain responsible for sexual arousal.

She looked at him and grinned. "Yes, Sir."

Back at their table, Adam sat down on the sofa and indicated that he wanted her to kneel by his feet. She slid as gracefully as she could down without hesitation and felt a flutter of excitement as she did so.

Adam leaned down and kissed her hard on the mouth. "I'm taking you down to the dungeon tonight and I've got a funny feeling you're going to enjoy it," he said, his voice low and husky.

Dungeon? The bottom dropped out of her stomach as fear took a firm grip on her. She'd forgotten about that place.

Adam chuckled. "I'm going to push your limits a bit tonight. I want to banish your demons before our little chat later, but first I think we need to re-establish your place."

Her brain picked out certain words and kept them spinning around in her head—'dungeon', 'push limits', 'chat later'. *Shit!*

He grabbed her hair and forced her to look up at him. "Stop thinking, Rachel. You are mine to do with as I see fit, do you understand?"

Despite her nervousness, she found herself responding to his words and the worry slowly started ebbing away to be replaced with that lovely gooey feeling she always seemed to get from being in a submissive headspace.

He jerked her hair slightly, waiting for her answer.

"Yes, Sir," she whispered.

"I'll expect you to follow strict protocol when we go down to the dungeon. You will not have permission to speak unless I ask you a direct question."

The gooey tingles started swirling around in her stomach now and she relaxed further into her submission. Oh yes, this was what it was all about.

"If I require you to speak, you will address me as Master. You will keep your eyes lowered at all times and, above all, you will obey me without question." His voice was in full Dom mode, firm, commanding and uncompromising.

The swirling in her tummy now reached her head and her whole body melted as she gave in to the dizzying effects of her submissive desires. She groaned as the tingles made their way down to her groin and teased her pussy, which started pulsing with need.

"Rachel, look at me."

She managed to focus her eyes on him and smiled. God she loved this man, who took everything he wanted from her, demanding her complete and utter surrender. Was this what it might be like as his slave? A shiver ran though her body at the thought.

"I need to warn you about the dungeons. Edge play is permitted down there, and there will be scenes going on that may disturb you. Don't forget that no matter how extreme things may seem, the same rule applies as up here—safe, sane and consensual. You will need to trust me not to harm you, but I will push your boundaries, do you understand?"

She was about to make a joke about Adam using the word 'Boundaries', but the warning in his voice sent a fresh shiver of fear through her instead. "Yes, Sir," she whispered again.

Adam reached down between her legs and stroked her along her labia. His fingers slid easily into her pussy and there was a wicked glint in his eyes as he held up the glistening finger and said, "I can see that I'm going to have fun with you tonight. Now, listen carefully. We're going to do a bit of role play downstairs. I seem to remember a discussion we had about you enjoying the act of being punished."

A bolt of lightning shot through her body and hit her clit so hard she actually jerked slightly from his words. Adam grinned and returned his hand to her pussy. Her face burned when he held up his saturated fingers.

"You will be the secretary and I will be your boss, sound familiar?" His eyes bore into hers, as if seeing every spark of arousal igniting with each word. "I will punish you for something you've done wrong. Now, let me see, what can you have done?" He put his finger on his chin and pretended to have a hard think. "Oh, yes. Let's pretend you've forgotten to order lunch in for a board meeting."

Shit, shit, shit. He was going to punish her for what had happened on Wednesday. *He must be seriously pissed off for him to wait until he can get me into the dungeon.* Images of whips and other terrifying implements of torture flashed through her mind and she swallowed nervously as she realized that this would be no role play. This was for real.

"Does that sound like a realistic scenario?" he asked with an evil grin on his face.

She couldn't stop her voice from faltering as she answered him, "Yes, Sir."

"Good. Remember, once we're downstairs, you must observe protocol. Come on."

He yanked the leash and she quickly stood up and stretched her legs which had gone slightly numb from her sitting on them for so long.

He led her to the top of the staircase and she stared down into the depths of hell with trepidation. It looked just as intimidating as it had before, only now even more so because she knew that this time she was actually going down there. With each step down, her pulse quickened as the sounds of the dungeon gradually grew louder. The screams and cries of pain, which merged with the sounds of Marilyn Manson, had a different quality to them, darker and way more intense than upstairs in the playrooms.

At the bottom, Adam pushed open a heavy wooden door and she found herself in a huge room. It was dark with only minimal lighting, mostly from red bulbs hidden in the ceiling. She held her breath as she gazed around, trying to take it all in. It was packed full of people in various stages of play — some people were strung up and being whipped by their Doms, and some poor subs were trapped in medieval looking stocks, whilst others were locked in cages. There was a massive wooden wheel against one wall with straps attached to it as well as several St. Andrew's crosses and spanking benches.

The sounds and smells were similar to those upstairs, but more intense. The smell of sex still hung heavily in the air, but there was something else, a smell of fear. Rachel jumped as an anguished scream reached her ears and she turned to see a mean-looking woman dressed head to toe in latex, hitting a man with a stick. Each time the stick made contact with the man's skin, the sound of electricity buzzed through the air and little sparks actually flew off his body. Rachel shuddered as the man howled and jerked, then quickly looked away.

On the other side of the room, a woman was strapped to a long table. She was writhing in agony as a large man poured burning hot wax over her nipples. Although there was no doubt that the woman was in a lot of pain, the look of pure ecstasy on her face told her that she loved every minute of it. *Rather her than me*, she thought with an uncomfortable shudder.

Adam pulled her leash and she followed him across the room. A large archway led through to a narrow corridor which was lined with rooms, similar to the ones upstairs, each with a theme. They passed a medical room, a prison cell and a school room, all buzzing with activity, until they came to an empty office and Adam stopped.

"Wait here until I call you to come in," he said in her ear, then left her to walk over to a large desk by the back wall.

As she watched him sit down on the office chair, images of their real office sprang to mind, and reminded her that she really was his secretary and he the boss. Whatever he wanted to do to her tonight was clearly something he couldn't do at the office. She swallowed nervously. Why would he wait until he had her in the dungeon? Was it because she might scream too loudly? *Fuck.*

She considered turning and getting the hell out of there, but just as she battled with her conscience, she heard Adam's familiar voice. "Miss Porter, get in here, *now*."

Her legs were trembling so much that she couldn't move for a moment, but one look at Adam's impatient face thankfully brought them back to life and she stepped slowly into the realistic looking office.

"What happened to our lunch today?" he barked, not dissimilar to the way he sometimes spoke at work.

"I…er…" She didn't know what to say. Was he talking about what really happened or did he want her to make something up?

"Speak up, girl," he shouted, losing patience.

"Er, sorry. I forgot to confirm the order, Sir," she stuttered.

Adam's face darkened. "Who?"

Shit. "Sorry, I mean, Master."

"You forgot?" he drawled.

"Yes, Sir… Master." She wanted to remind him that she'd heroically saved the day, but she had a feeling he wouldn't be interested in that little detail.

"Oh dear." He smiled darkly. "You naughty, naughty girl." He stood up and walked around the desk to stand in front of her. "On your knees," he snapped.

She immediately sank down, her heartbeat quickening as she did so.

"What happens to naughty girls, Miss Porter?"

Ohhh shit… She grew weak as desire flared inside her. She hadn't thought she'd get involved enough with this to get off, but damn it if she wasn't getting hornier by the second.

"They get punished, Master," she said, through a shiver.

He towered over her, but she kept her eyes lowered as he'd told her to. Shit, what was he going to do?

"Yes, Miss Porter, they do." He grabbed her by the hair and yanked it back so she was forced to look up into his face. A deep shudder went through her body again, tightening her stomach muscles and quickening her pulse. There was a dull ache between her legs, an ache that needed to be taken care of, and she unconsciously let her hand wander to the sensitive area.

Before she could even blink, Adam slapped her hand away and yanked her hair harder. "You will *not* touch yourself, is that clear?" His voice boomed in her ears, angry and authoritative.

"Yes, Master." Her voice came out as a whimper, and the ache became stronger.

"Get up," growled Adam, stepping back and crossing his arms.

She quickly scrambled back onto her feet and stood facing him, waiting for him to order her to do whatever he wished. Despite her reservations about coming down to the dungeon and her fears about Adam's motives for the impending punishment, Rachel couldn't deny the fact that she was enjoying this sexy role play scenario. She was so horny she would gladly have humped his leg if he'd let her, and the promise of a spanking or flogging filled her with such anticipation that she couldn't stop her body from trembling with excitement.

"Strip!" he commanded, not taking his eyes off her. She started fumbling with the buttons on her blouse, but something about the look in his eyes scared her a bit and her trembling fingers became clumsy as she awkwardly tried to undo the remaining buttons.

"Let me help you," growled Adam gruffly. He reached forward and ripped the blouse open.

A couple of buttons flew across the room and Rachel jumped as he roughly pulled the offending material from her body and threw it on the floor. He stepped back and nodded at her skirt. She quickly unzipped it and let it drop to the floor, leaving her completely naked.

Adam stared silently at her, devouring her body as she stood helpless and uncertain in a room where anyone passing could look in. She didn't dare turn around to see if she had an audience—and anyway, she'd rather not know. She focused instead on Adam, who was still staring at her with that same look that sent shivers of fear and excitement through her body. There was something wild, almost animalistic, about the deeply intense look in his eyes, the lust merging with something dark and slightly sinister.

Then he broke the gaze and nodded toward the large wooden desk. "Lean across it," he ordered, firmly taking hold of her arm. He marched her up to the desk until she stood flush against it then pushed her roughly down so she was leaning across it the way she had in the boardroom, her head turned so her cheek was resting on the cool wood.

He grabbed both her wrists and pulled them over her head until they were completely stretched out, then attached her cuffs to chains secured to the end of the desk. With her legs pressed against the edge and her body firmly against the top, she was completely immobile, but Adam nevertheless attached her ankle cuffs to more chains so that she was securely restrained.

Suddenly the sounds of the club became muffled and her vision blurry as her arousal took on a new dimension. She was about to be punished, in public, whilst tethered to a desk by her imaginary boss. Not only that, but she was to be punished for a real crime by her real boss, bringing an exciting, but dangerous dynamic into the mix. Suddenly the reality of the situation hit home. Was he going to hurt her? Would he whip her till she begged for mercy? He had after all said he was going to push her boundaries. Her breath caught in her throat and her body stiffened in panic. Oh, God, she couldn't do this.

She immediately felt Adam's hand, firm yet gentle, rub her back. He leaned down, kissed the back of her neck and whispered in her ear, "Rachel, I won't harm you. What's your safe word?"

Safe word. Oh yes, she had a safe word. "Red, Master," she whispered back.

"Good girl. Use it if you need to."

But she knew he wanted to push her limits and that he would be disappointed if she took the easy way out, and besides, she deserved the punishment. Her acknowledgment sent fresh shocks of lust through her body. God, what was it about being punished that turned her on so much? She resolved not to use her safe word, no matter what. He must be getting pretty fed up with her, not only because of what had happened with the lunch, but because she was being such a wimp about committing to him. Well, she'd take her punishment and make him proud of her, then he may be more understanding when they had their 'chat' later.

The first thing she felt was the soft fronds of a flogger caressing her back. *Hmm...nice.* She relaxed a little as the fronds kissed her skin with light flicks. This was more like a massage. She knew she could take the sting of a flogger, even when he hit her quite hard with it. So she closed her eyes and sighed contentedly as the flogger progressively got harder.

She didn't know how long he flogged her for, but when he stopped, she moaned in disappointment. Her skin was warm and tingly and her head felt very similar. She was on the edge of subspace again, the pleasure of the flogger mixed with the excitement of being punished, pushing her to the delicious heights she had only recently discovered. Then she felt two fingers push through her opening and she purred like a kitten as they probed her throbbing, wet pussy.

But, to her disappointment, the fingers withdrew all too quickly and instead something cold and hard ran along her back. Her eyes snapped open again and she saw that Adam had walked to the side of the desk so she could see him. She swallowed nervously when she saw that he was holding a thin stick in his hand. His eyes were gleaming with excitement and his lips curled into a dangerous grin when he must have seen the recognition in her wide eyes.

"Now, Miss Porter, let's get back to the matter of your punishment. Naughty girls get their bottoms spanked, but you've been very naughty so we're going to go one better. You'll receive ten strokes of this beautiful rattan cane and you will count each one. Do you understand?"

"Yes, Master," she whispered. She'd heard that canes could be more painful than some whips. A flashback to Amelia's backside, criss-crossed with angry red welts brought tears to her eyes and she shut them tightly as she braced herself for impact.

The first stroke was so light she barely felt it. "One." Was that it?

The next one was also fairly light, leaving only a little sting in its wake. "Two." She let go of her trepidation a bit as she waited for the third stroke which, although harder, still didn't really hurt that much either. She grinned to herself as her body relaxed some more. Was this really all there was to it? The fourth stroke, again, was fairly gentle and she frowned. Amazingly she actually wanted a bit more pain, something to send her into the lovely headspace she'd been in before. She groaned in the hope that Adam would get the message.

"Argh," she gasped, as the fifth stroke came down much harder than the others. Her arse stung. *Shit, that really hurts.*

"Count, Rachel," growled Adam, and slapped the sore spot on her arse.

"Ow. Five," she cried, just as the sixth came down.

At first it didn't seem that bad, but a split second later, a line of fire seared across her skin and she cried out in shock as the pain gripped her by the throat. She tried to move her body, but she was so securely restrained that her attempt was futile.

She couldn't speak, the muscles in her throat tightened so much that she could barely breathe, let alone utter any words. Fuck, this was too much. *Stop,* she thought to herself, *I need him to stop, I can't take anymore,* but the desire to please him was stronger, and she remained silent.

"Count, Rachel, or we start again."

Adam's voice found its way into her brain and she just about managed to gasp, "Six."

Then number seven hit and she screamed in agony as fire exploded across the back of her thigh. She raised herself onto her tiptoes as if that would take away some of the pain, but of course it didn't. Enough, she couldn't do this. She needed him to stop, *now.* "Red," she gasped, through her tears, but to her horror nothing came out. Her vocal chords seemed to have stopped working and all that came out was a raspy croak which she knew Adam wouldn't hear. Oh, no, she wouldn't survive another one, but Adam didn't respond and lifted his arm again. "Red, red, red," she cried, as she braced herself for number eight.

Chapter Seven

Rachel looked up into Adam's face as he carried her upstairs, away from the sounds of the dungeon. She couldn't read his expression, but it didn't look good. His eyes were dark and the frown that had narrowed his brow earlier seemed even more deeply ingrained now. Was he angry? Disappointed?

She had so wanted to make him proud of her, to show him that she would take whatever punishment he chose to dish out, to prove her submission to him. But she'd failed, safe worded at the very first hurdle. Thank Heaven, he'd stopped when he had though, she couldn't bear to think what it would have felt like if he'd continued hitting her with that cane.

She closed her eyes and savored the comfort of being in his arms—it probably wouldn't last for much longer. When she opened her eyes again, she found they were in the aftercare lounge, her favorite place. Adam placed her gently onto a plump cushion, making sure she was on her side.

"I'm sorry," she whispered, as fresh tears sprung from her eyes. Why hadn't she held on just a little bit longer, she'd only had three more strokes to take—three!

"You shouldn't be sorry. Come on, rest now."

Adam's voice soothed her. Her eyes felt heavy, she was so sleepy. No, she'd screwed up enough lately, the last thing he needed was for her to fall asleep on him. She forced them open again and saw Adam leaning over her to inspect her backside. "You've got a couple of pretty pink stripes across your ass," he said solemnly.

Was that all she had to show for her agony? She didn't have the energy for words though, so she just smiled weakly up at him and closed her eyes again.

"Luke's going to come and sit with you while I sort a few things here and then I'm taking you home." Although there was no anger his voice, she was devastated at his words. She didn't want to go home—she wanted to stay with Adam. She nearly begged him to let her stay with him, but she'd already learnt that antagonizing an angry Dom wasn't the cleverest thing a sub could do, so she remained silent.

She was barely aware of Luke sitting with her. The last two nights had been tough. She had been fretting about Adam ever since the board meeting on Wednesday and had lain awake for hours, unable to get to sleep. When she had eventually managed to drop off, her restless dreams had woken her soon after, leaving her feeling more drained than before.

She was exhausted and, without realizing it, she drifted off to sleep briefly. When she woke a little while later, she found Luke's handsome face smiling down at her. "You all right?" he asked.

She nodded and managed a smile. Luke was such a lovely guy, every bit as dominant as Adam, but with a slightly softer side. Why couldn't she have fallen for him instead of Adam? Life would have been so much easier.

Fifty minutes later, she was snuggled up to Adam as Rob made his way through the gloomy, wet London streets. Her head was resting on his shoulder and they traveled in silence, but Rachel's thoughts were anything but silent. They were spinning furiously around her head, tormenting her for being such a pathetic wimp. He must be so disappointed in her. She closed her eyes in shame. "I'm sorry I safe worded," she said suddenly, her voice barely a whisper.

Adam stiffened and pulled her closer to him. "Hey, never be sorry for using your safe word, it's there to stop anything that gets too intense or painful. You were right to use it," he said quietly.

She lifted her head to look at him, but it was too dark to see his expression.

"I'm sorry I hurt you," he said, his voice now heavy with regret.

"Oh, Adam, it's my fault. I'm so sorry," she cried. "Please don't take me home, I want to be with you."

"Who said anything about taking you home?" he said with a frown.

"You did. Before, in the club."

"I didn't mean take you back to your home," he laughed, "I meant *my* home."

When they arrived back in Hampstead, they were greeted by Thor and Freya. Adam led Rachel through to the kitchen, put some milk on the stove and fed the hungry cats whilst the milk warmed.

"You're going to drink this hot chocolate and then you're going upstairs to bed. To *sleep*," he added with a grin as her eyes lit up. "Don't worry—I fully intend to fuck you senseless in the morning. And then we talk, okay?"

She nodded mutely and took the mug of hot chocolate he held out to her. Yes, sleep was what she needed right now. After a good night's sleep, she would hopefully be able to think a bit more coherently when she woke. She barely acknowledged Adam pulling the duvet over her or kissing her softly on her lips, for within about a second of her head hitting the pillow, she was asleep.

* * * *

The first thing she became aware of as she slowly emerged from her sleep the following morning, was her arms being raised above her head. Then, something clicked in her left ear followed by one in her right ear. Her legs were spread open, her right ankle secured to the corner of one side of the bed and her left leg to the other side. She still had her eyes closed, but she knew exactly what was going on—she was naked and spread-eagled on the bed, tethered so there would be no escape. A surge of heat warmed her body and she opened her eyes to look into Adam's smoldering eyes.

"Good morning, sexy," he said, his voice husky from sleep. "I'm about to worship your body and all you have to do is lie back and think of England."

"There are other things I'd rather think about," she giggled.

"Sssh, you don't have permission to speak or to come until I tell you otherwise." Adam's voice was deep, sexy and so very commanding.

She was already wet and could feel the subtle breeze in the room tickle her naked, exposed pussy.

Adam straddled her and placed a blindfold over her eyes. "I don't want anything to distract you," he murmured.

He started by nibbling her ear, making her giggle as his warm breath tickled her. Then he planted lots of light kisses over her face and neck, the kisses slowly becoming hotter as his lips were replaced by his tongue. He licked his way down to her breasts, smoothing over the goosebumps that covered her body with each delicious shiver he induced.

"Hmm," she moaned as his tongue found her nipple. It hardened in his mouth as he sucked on it, and little shivers of electricity rippled through her body in response. He focused on her breasts for a long time—sucking, licking and nibbling until her nipples were so tight she almost couldn't bear it—almost!

She tugged slightly on the restraints and a surge of excitement charged through her when she couldn't move away from his touch. The low, gentle buzzing between her legs notched up a level to a delicious throb and she sighed happily as there was nothing she could do except lay back and enjoy every moment.

His tongue eventually left her nipples and trailed down her stomach, sending a fresh trail of goosebumps to the surface of her tingling skin.

She missed his fingers though. Up until now he had only used his mouth on her and she was starting to feel strong urges to have something inside her. His cock would be perfect, but his fingers would do nicely if he wasn't ready to fuck her just yet. She arched her pelvis slightly, hoping he'd get the message, but his fingers remained frustratingly elusive and her pussy remained wet, but empty.

His tongue moved farther down, over her soft, shaved mound then, finally, down to her pussy which was, by now, screaming for attention. His fingers gently pulled her labia aside before he ran his tongue over the soft, velvety flesh around her opening to her vagina.

"Oh, please," she whimpered, although she wasn't sure what it was she was asking for. Was it more of this wonderful, slow teasing, or was it because she needed him inside her? Both, she decided. She wanted both, she wanted it all and she wanted more.

When his tongue finally found its way inside her, a feeling of such delirium filled her that it actually brought on the beginnings of an orgasm. She felt beautiful, safe, adored and she never wanted it to end. The feelings intensified and she couldn't stop herself from clamping onto his tongue, but then, just before she reached that point of no return, he pulled away.

"Ohhh," she groaned, in frustration. "Please don't stop."

"Did I say you could come?" he asked, his voice sounding hoarse.

"No, Sir. Sorry." Damn him, she had been so close.

He waited until her body settled down a bit before starting again, this time paying more attention to her clit. He flicked it with his tongue, over and over until she didn't think she could bear it any longer. She needed release. "Oh, yes," she whispered as the telltale waves started building again. He carried on, ruthlessly bringing her back to the brink and, once again just as she was about to come, he pulled away.

"Not yet, Rachel."

His voice, although husky and sexy, told her he was serious. *Bastard!*

Again he waited until her body had calmed down then started again, only this time, he inserted his finger into her pussy at the same time as licking her clit. It took all of two minutes before she was back up on the edge of the cliff again, ready to tumble over, and yet again the bastard stopped just as she was about to fall off.

"Pleeaase," she cried, now so desperate that tears were filling her eyes under the blindfold. "Please let me come." The frustration was making her whole body ache for release and she groaned as it shuddered with need.

"Are you begging, Rachel?" He had her, she knew it. He controlled every last bit of her body, her mind and her pleasure and she surrendered completely as she welcomed his omnipotence.

"Yes, Sir. I'm begging. Please, please may I come?"

"Okay, but tell me that you love me, first."

What? "That's not fair," she gasped.

"Look, we both know you love me so there's no point in acting all coy. Tell me you love me—admit it, and I'll let you come."

She could tell he was serious. Damn him, if he was so sure she loved him, why did he have to force her to say it? But she knew why. By making her say the words aloud, he would come one step closer to breaking down the steel wall she had erected around her heart.

"All right, you bastard, I love you," she cried, her body tensing as she heard herself say the words aloud.

"Now say it without calling me a bastard."

Bastard! "I love you," she whispered, finally acknowledging what she had known all along.

"Good girl," he whispered back. "I love you too." His voice, although still hoarse with sexual tension, now held a tone of something else. The tears behind the blindfold finally spilled as she recognized the love in his voice, and the relief.

"You can come now, baby," he said, and clamped his mouth around her aching clit. He pulled it and sucked it hard while with two fingers fucked her pussy until she started seeing stars in the darkness.

"Argh," she screamed as she finally went over the edge, her body racking violently with every glorious wave. He inserted his tongue into her pussy again and she cried out as fresh waves pulsed through her shaking body.

Finally, when her body was completely still, Adam moved away and pulled off the blindfold. "I knew it." He grinned and kissed her hard on the lips so she could taste her own arousal.

"You bribed me," she said, with a feigned frown, although she knew he could tell it wasn't real. As if she would be capable of frowning after an orgasm like that.

"Tell me you meant it," he demanded, as if needing to hear it again before he really believed it.

"Yes, I meant it." She looked up into his eyes and saw the love reflecting back at her. Then they became darker as they filled with lust again and, without another word, he reached up and unclipped her wrists. Once he'd released her ankles, he pulled her up and flipped her onto her front.

"On your hands and knees," he growled, sounding once again every bit the demanding Dom she loved so much. She rose as ordered and was rewarded with a fresh wave of arousal as his cock probed her slick entrance from behind. With one strong thrust, he drove into her, filling her completely.

"Oh, yes," she cried, as he grabbed her hair and held her in place. He was fucking her so hard, she could barely catch her breath as he repeatedly drove his cock into her, faster and harder every time. Oh, how she loved this, the feeling of being taken, overpowered and completely dominated in every sense.

When his cock swelled inside her, she knew he wasn't far off coming and her own excitement escalated. He drove into her, rubbing against her G-spot and she knew it was only a matter of time before she would succumb. Thankfully, just as she teetered on the edge, she heard him growl, "Come now," and everything blurred around her. They came together, their bodies in perfect sync with each other.

It was several minutes before either of them could speak. They just lay in each other's arms, hot, sweaty and deliciously sated.

"Let me hear you say it again," he said softly.

"I love you," she whispered, and fell into a blissful sleep.

She woke a little while later to find Adam standing next to the bed, looking down at her. He'd just come out of the shower, tiny water droplets hung from his hair and clung to his skin. She wanted to lick them off and unconsciously ran her tongue over her lips.

"Good morning, sleepy head." He smiled, his dimples sending butterflies fluttering through her belly. "I'm going to prepare breakfast while you shower and dress." He leaned over her and planted a light kiss on her forehead. It was an affectionate, gentle gesture. *No more sex then?*

* * * *

Half an hour later, she was enjoying the pancakes and scrambled eggs Adam had made. The cats were curled up in their favorite place, a large beam of sunlight near the window. She sipped her coffee and wondered if things could be any more perfect.

"We need to talk."

Adam's voice broke her little bubble of contentedness and she realized that this was probably going to be the 'talk' where he told her how pissed off he'd been with her then he'd probably give her an ultimatum — be his slave or leave. The trouble was, although she loved him with all her heart, she still wasn't prepared to give up her independence and freedom, even for him.

Her heart sank and started hammering furiously. She looked away for a moment and tried not to appear too nervous as she waited for him to speak.

"I'm sorry I hurt you last night," he said quietly. "I thought you were enjoying it. I was trying to build the intensity up slowly so it wouldn't be such a shock for you. I didn't hear you say the safe word at first, it was only when I saw the way you were reacting that I stopped and listened more carefully."

"But you did stop. In fact, you were so in tune with me that you stopped before you even heard me calling my safe word. It's not your fault, Adam, it's mine. I'm the one who should be apologizing to you. I deserved that punishment and had resolved to take it for you no matter what, but I wimped out as soon as it became too intense." She could hear the remorse in her voice and hoped he would hear it too and forgive her.

"What do you mean you deserved the punishment? It was role play, Rachel." Adam's sharp voice interrupted her, leaving her momentarily speechless.

"I...er... Well, I thought you were just using the role play scenario to make it more formal." She faltered slightly when she saw the frown on his face. Shit, this was coming out all wrong. "I mean, you used what happened about lunch on Wednesday as the reason for the punishment and I thought you meant it for real..." She trailed off, feeling suddenly very uncertain. Had she got it wrong?

"Rachel, let me make one thing very clear. Whatever takes place at work, remains at work. I will never punish you for anything you may or may not do in the office, at least not seriously. Do you understand?"

She nodded.

"I thought you'd find the whole scene rather amusing," he said, looking a bit affronted. "Let me also put you straight on another thing. I'm damned proud of the way you dealt with things on Wednesday. You remained calm and sorted the problem quickly and easily. No one in that boardroom, except for me, knew what had happened and that's because of your unflappable and prompt actions. Why would I punish you for that?"

Rachel shrugged. "I'm sorry. You were so mad after the meeting and then you flew out to Amsterdam without talking to me and I thought..."

Adam laughed. "You thought I went to Amsterdam because I was mad at you for rescuing the lunch?"

The heat of a blush stained her cheeks. Now that he'd put it like that...

"The reason I had to fly out to Amsterdam at such short notice was because Lord Granville drew something to my attention during the meeting. It turns out that one of our employees in the Dutch office has been trying to sabotage our client accounts. I found out that one of our rivals had planted him to make several serious mistakes on our biggest account and he would then divert the client to them." Adam's face showed the strain of the last couple of days as he spoke and Rachel's heart went out to him. She had, as usual, assumed the worst and not stopped to think that there could be a perfectly good reason why he had acted the way he had. And, instead of being supportive of him, she'd let her own insecurities stop her from giving him that support. Mandy had been right to smack her.

"Did you find out who it was?" she asked in a small voice.

"Yes, it was easy to trace things back to him. Needless to say, he's out on his ear and facing serious charges. I spent the rest of the trip trying to win back the confidence of our client." That explained the exhaustion she'd seen on his face.

"Did you manage it?" she asked, and reached for his hand across the table.

He nodded. "Yes, when I'd explained what had happened they were very understanding and have resumed their business with us."

"I'm so glad." She squeezed his hand and smiled.

"Now, forget about that, that wasn't what I wanted to talk about. Tell me how you felt last night during the scene. I want to know where it started to go wrong so we can avoid it happening again. Was it purely the pain?"

She shuddered slightly as she remembered the fiery sting of the cane. "Yes, it was mostly the pain, it was just too much."

"You were turned on though," he said matter-of-factly.

"Yes, but like last time, it was the fact that I was being punished that turned me on so much. I liked the feel of the flogger and even the first strokes of the cane, but when you hit harder, it became too much." Oddly enough though, now that she was thinking back to it, she did sort of like it in a perverse sort of way. She had to admit that even though it had hurt so badly, she had been very turned on at the same time.

Was it just the punishment scenario that had aroused her so much, or had the pain played a part in it?

Adam must have read her thoughts because he said, "I think you like pain more than you realize. It could have been the fact that you thought the punishment was for real that made you tense up, which would have made it far more painful for you. If you were truly relaxed and warmed up, you might find you'll enjoy it." A slow smile spread across his face as he added, "And, if you don't, I'll just have to keep the cane for real punishments in the future as a deterrent."

The blood drained from Rachel's face. Was he serious? She remembered what he'd said about punishments not being about pleasure and felt a frisson of fear as she studied his face, looking for a sign that he had been joking. But his face remained deadpan and she resolved never to risk pissing him off so much that he might keep his word.

Chapter Eight

Adam grinned at her across the breakfast table. No doubt he had seen the look of fear that must have shown on her face. "Don't worry, I'll never go beyond your limits. Going back to what happened on Wednesday," he said, solemnly, "I must take some responsibility for it."

Rachel laughed. "Adam, how could it possibly be your fault that I forgot to confirm the order?"

"If I hadn't distracted you, you probably wouldn't have forgotten. I normally never mix business with pleasure and now that I have, we're both suffering the consequences. The trouble is, I don't seem to be able to resist you," he said, with a sexy smile playing on his lips. A memory flashed through her mind of the fierce and angry Adam Stone who had scared the living daylights out of her on her first day working for him and yet, here he was, admitting he was partly to blame. She was glad that he had distracted her, even if that meant making mistakes that would normally have gotten her fired.

She had intended to wait for Joanne to tell him about her new job, but suddenly now seemed as good a time as any to mention it. "I might have a solution to that problem," she said nervously.

Adam raised his eyebrows. "Oh?"

"Well, you see…" She coughed slightly to clear her throat. "Joanne Baker has offered me a job." There, she'd said it. "Only after Lucy's replacement starts, of course," she added hastily.

She held her breath as she waited for the imminent explosion but he just smiled and squeezed her hand.

"Good, I'm glad."

"You don't sound surprised."

"Joanne had mentioned that she wanted you to work for her one day. She's very impressed with your ability with numbers. She asked if I would have any objection if she hired you once the new girl starts. I'm really pleased for you, Rachel. And for me. It'll be so much easier not having you under my nose all the time to torment me."

"Me torment *you*?" she laughed.

Adam laughed back and leaned over the table to kiss her. "Congratulations," he said. "You deserve it. I didn't tell you before, but the new girl can start sooner than expected, so you can start your new job next month if you like. To be honest, I wasn't too pleased when HR told me about Lucy's replacement starting early because I was enjoying you so much, but it looks like it's worked out for the best. Maybe I can get some work done now," he added with a chuckle.

Adam rose from his chair and put some more coffee on. "Look, there is something else we need to discuss, but I've got to go into the office this afternoon. Why don't you go shopping while I'm gone, I shouldn't be long. Tonight, we're going back to Boundaries, and then I want you to stay with me for the rest of the weekend. I want to spend as much time with you as possible."

He may not think that once they'd had their chat later, she thought silently, but smiled and forced herself to look happy at the idea of a bit of leisurely shopping.

* * * *

Rachel had spent the afternoon browsing the boutiques in Hampstead High Street. They were way out of her price range, but it never hurt to dream. She'd had a coffee in a cute little coffee shop and had had a freshly made crepe outside a pub. She was relaxed and had enjoyed her afternoon, but now that she was walking back to Adam's house, the nervous flutters in her stomach started niggling again. Tonight, they would have the talk that would determine their future together. Would he compromise and offer to give her a little more freedom than other slaves might have, or would she cave in and agree to everything he demanded because she was so scared of losing him?

I've got to stand my ground, she thought determinedly. Mandy was right. If neither of them were happy it would only destroy their relationship in the end and that was unthinkable. But losing him now was unthinkable too. Oh why couldn't he just be a nice, normal vanilla guy? But she knew she wouldn't have him any other way. If he'd been vanilla, he wouldn't have owned a kink club and have orchestrated their meeting there for a start.

And anyway, she loved the kink. How she could have spent all these years not knowing she was into kinky sex was beyond her. Oh sure, she'd had dreams about being tied up and spanked, but surely most people had those, didn't they? Whatever happened with Adam tonight though, she knew she'd never be able to go back to a vanilla relationship. She loved the rough sex, that lovely submissive melty feeling she got from being dominated and the delicious pain that came with it.

Adam still wasn't back when she let herself into the house, so she ran a bath and settled into it with a glass of chilled pinot grigio from his fridge. She sank back and closed her eyes, her body relaxing in the hot, bubbly water. She wondered what Adam had planned for her tonight. Hopefully he'd want to play a bit before tackling the TPE issue, and her body heated at the possibility of a good flogging.

She was just fantasizing about being strapped naked to a spanking bench, when the bathroom door opened with a creak and a moment later she felt Adam's thumb rub over her soapy nipple. Hmm, nice. He pinched it hard. Oh yes, even nicer.

"I'd love to jump in with you and fuck you senseless," he said. She shivered slightly in the warm water. "But, we've got to get ready. I'm opening up tonight, so we need to get there early again. We can have a quiet drink before the members arrive. It'll give us a chance to talk before it gets busy."

Oh, yes. 'The talk'. There went any chance of a nice flogging before he dumped her then.

"By the way, I've left a present for you on the bed," he said as he continued teasing her nipples. "See you downstairs."

She sighed as he left the bathroom and headed downstairs. God, she was going to miss him. At that moment, she came very close to giving in and letting him demand anything he wanted from her. She climbed out of the bath and absently rubbed herself dry, completely lost in her thoughts. A sense of doom seemed to follow her through to the bedroom. Would this be their last night together?

When she saw the dress he'd left for her, she gasped, her gloomy reverie briefly forgotten. It was a very expensive looking designer evening dress and was made from the softest high quality leather she had ever felt. She slipped it on and studied herself critically in the mirror. The skirt reached the ground, but had a long slit all the way up the side, exposing most of her right thigh when she moved. The bodice was tight and both pinched her waist in and pushed her breasts up. The front of the bodice was decorated in tiny, twinkling rhinestones and looked like something a Hollywood actress would wear to the Oscars, except for the fact that it was leather, of course. It must have cost a bloody fortune.

Adam whistled when he came back into the bedroom and, in response, she did a flirty little twirl for him. She felt beautiful tonight, which wasn't something she experienced very often. The dress fitted like a glove and she guessed he might have had it made especially for her. Her legs were bare and looked long and sleek in the high stiletto shoes he'd bought to go with the outfit. Her makeup was subtle, with pale foundation and just a little smoky eyeliner and mascara on her eyes, but her blood red lipstick was bold and striking in comparison.

"You look gorgeous," he murmured, and ran his hand over the soft flesh of her bulging cleavage.

"Thank you." She smiled as he kissed the back of her neck. She'd put her hair up into a classic chignon exposing her slender neck to Adam's lips.

Regrettably, his lips left her neck all too soon. "Come on, Rob's waiting."

She greeted the driver warmly as they climbed into the car. Although he wasn't the most communicative person she'd ever met, he made her feel at ease and she appreciated that.

As Rob drove them through the streets of London, Rachel stared distractedly out of the window, silently rehearsing her speech for later. She jumped when, suddenly, he leaned toward her, ran his hand up the inside of her thigh and playfully pinched her clit. "Oh!" she cried. Her body responded immediately and when he took her mouth in a hard, forceful kiss, she forgot all about her speech and could only think about Adam's finger, which was now seeking its way through her wet folds.

There was no gentle teasing this time, he finger-fucked her hard and fast and she whimpered into his mouth as her body begged for more. He brought her close, so close to orgasm, but never actually let her come. Instead he pulled away and growled in her ear, "Enough. I want you nice and horny for tonight. Get on the floor."

Oh, yes! Her blood heated as his order sent shivers of lust through her body. She slid silently and obediently to the floor then knelt between his legs. When she reached for his zipper she smiled in the darkness when she saw how hard he was. She eased his solid cock out and leaned forward to kiss the tip before taking him into her mouth.

He let out a groan and a surge of pleasure soared through her that she had the power to evoke such a strong reaction so quickly. She loved to do this for him, loved the taste of him and the feel of the thick veins throbbing in her mouth. She pulled away slightly and ran her tongue along the length of his cock, first along the top then the bottom before teasing him with her teeth at the bulging tip. She could taste the salty pre-cum and her pussy clenched as she became increasingly excited.

Then he took hold of her head, holding her in place. She prayed he'd run them roughly through her hair and pull it hard, but he didn't, which was probably just as well considering the effort she'd gone to with that damned chignon. But his hands were enough to make her feel controlled and she groaned in pleasure as he pushed her head down, forcing her to take more of him into her mouth and throat.

She sucked, licked and massaged his cock with her tongue and when he pushed her head farther down, she relaxed her throat muscles enough to take the whole length of him inside her. She couldn't breathe — he had complete control over her, even over her next breath. He kept her head down until finally, just as she started struggling for air, he released her and let her gasp huge breaths of air back into her lungs.

"Get up," he said, his voice low and husky.

"But…"

"You don't want to spoil that lovely makeup," he said, with a hint of a smile in his voice. "Straddle me and ride me till I come inside you. I want my cum to trickle down your legs as you walk into Boundaries."

"Yes, Sir." She smiled and climbed up. As she hitched one leg over him and eased herself onto his hard cock, she was amazed at how little she was bothered now by the fact that Rob could be watching. She sighed as she slid deeper onto him until she couldn't go any farther. He was so big, so hard, and the feeling of being filled with his incredible shaft gave her such a thrill that it made her ride him with complete abandon. Faster and harder, deeper and rougher, she rode him until he groaned and pulled her down hard by her shoulders, forcing her to keep still while he filled her with his hot cum.

"Don't you dare come," he growled, when he was able to catch his breath again. "I want you desperate and begging for your orgasms tonight."

"Yes, Sir," she hissed and forced herself to repress her pleasure before she lost control completely. When she eventually climbed off him, her clit was throbbing so much that it brought tears to her eyes and when a few drops of his cum slipped out of her pussy and ran down her thigh, she gave a little sob of frustration.

By the time they pulled up outside Boundaries, Adam had the smile of a satisfied man whilst Rachel had the glare of pent up frustration as her increased arousal at pleasuring Adam had gone unreleased.

"Be patient, sweet thing." He grinned, as he helped her out of the car. "It'll be worth the wait."

She scowled at him as she stepped away from the car and straightened the skirt of her dress. They made their way around to the back door and she watched sulkily as Adam unlocked it and switched off the alarm system.

"I've got to sort out a couple of things, but Chrissie will be here soon and she can take over. Then we talk."

Adam strode over to the bar and, as she followed him, warm moisture trickled down the inside of her thighs. But, instead of making her smile, it only brought tears to her eyes. This should have been such a sexy moment, but instead, she felt like she was about to be led to the gallows. He poured her a cola and kissed her softly before disappearing into the office, leaving her alone with her melancholic thoughts.

* * * *

She'd no idea how long he'd been gone for, but suddenly Adam gripped her shoulders and kissed her on the back of her neck.

"Chrissie's here now so we've got a bit of time alone. Do you want another drink?"

Yeah, a triple bloody brandy, she wanted to say, but shook her head instead.

"Are you all right?"

Rachel turned around and smiled at Adam. "I'm fine," she lied, and forced a cheerful smile onto her face. Adam didn't look convinced. She closed her eyes when he started gently massaging her shoulders but not from the enjoyment of his touch. She didn't want him to see the tears that were gathering behind her lids, so she kept them closed and tried to look like she was relaxing.

"You will get your release tonight, I promise," he whispered in her ear. "I want you to explode like a firework when I finally allow you to come."

She smiled again, still silent. If he wanted to think she was quiet because she was frustrated at not being allowed to come earlier then let him think that.

Her eyes ran over his body — shit, he looked hot. He was back in his leathers, his black T-shirt showing off his bulging muscles and tribal tattoos. He hadn't shaved, so his face was framed with sexy dark stubble and his hair was ruffled and unkempt. He looked every part the perfect Dom, in fact, he *was* the perfect Dom. If only he wanted her for who she was and not what she could never be.

He leaned forward and kissed the back of her neck again and it took all her strength to hold back the sob that threatened to give her away.

Her mind felt like it was spinning out of control, tormenting her with images of Adam's angry reaction when she told him she wouldn't agree to be his slave. She knew deep down that no matter how much she loved him, she wouldn't give in on this, but she also knew that he was a man that generally got what he wanted. It didn't bode well.

Why had she even agreed to come tonight? She'd known that this was on the cards and yet still she'd still obeyed him and, damn it, loved him. She knew why though. Until she heard him say the words out loud, there was still hope that they could come to some sort of mutual understanding.

It was at that moment she realized that she could never love anyone else but Adam Stone. If their relationship was to end tonight, if he was to leave her because she wouldn't agree to his demands, then she'd be single for the rest of her life, she knew that now. Another uncomfortable thought crossed her mind then. If she was so adamant that she wouldn't compromise, how could she hope that he might do so? *That smacks of double standards, Rachel Porter,* she scolded herself, and her heart sank even further with her acknowledgment that the end was inevitable.

A tear ran down Rachel's cheek, and Adam reached out and gently wiped it away.

"Hey," he said softly. "What's the matter?"

This was it. The moment she'd been dreading, and avoiding, but there was no avoiding it anymore. But now that the moment had come, she couldn't find the words she needed to explain how she felt. She loved him so very much and she needed him, but she could never be what he needed her to be. Why couldn't she just say it like that?

Adam's voice hardened slightly as he said, "There's something very serious I want to ask you tonight, but I know something's bothering you. You need to tell me what's wrong before we can go any further."

His face blurred as tears filled her eyes. Why couldn't he just be happy with what they had? Wasn't it enough? Anger suddenly replaced her sorrow as the unfairness of it all hit her. Why should she be the one to give everything up?

She stood up abruptly, scraping the chair back loudly in the silent club. "Fuck you, Adam," she shouted, unable to control herself anymore. All her pent up anger and frustration now boiled to the surface and started spilling over. But when she looked defiantly back at Adam, instead of seeing anger, she was shocked to see the look of stunned disbelief on his face, and suddenly all the anger drained out of her and the only thing she could think to do was run.

She turned and ran away from the bar as fast as she could. She didn't know where she was going, she didn't care, she just needed to get away from Adam before he broke her heart completely and destroyed the wonderful love they shared.

She ran blindly down across the room, feeling like a hunted rabbit, but just as she thought she'd escaped, a firm hand gripped her arm and threw her against the wall. She closed her eyes and screamed as hysteria gripped her, until she was pulled into strong arms and held with an iron grip.

Slowly, she pulled away and opened her eyes to find Adam glaring at her, not with anger she realized, but with concern. Suddenly, the last fight drained out of her and she resigned herself to the fact that she would never be able to resist his power over her.

Adam didn't say a word, he just led her back across the room, into the aftercare lounge, and sat her down on one of the sofas.

"Better now?" he asked, as he sat down next to her. His voice was calm, but the look in his eyes told her he was anything but calm.

She nodded slowly and took a deep breath.

"Good. Now tell me what the hell that was all about," he demanded.

The tears spilled then, and through the sobs, she was finally able to say what she so badly needed to say. "I can't be your slave, Adam. I love you so much, I really do, but I can't—*won't* give up my freedom."

"What the hell are you talking about?" growled Adam. He sounded genuinely shocked.

"I know you want another TPE and I really have tried to get my head around it. I've thought of nothing else, Adam, please believe me, but I can't do it. I love you so much and I'll do pretty much anything for you...except become your slave. I'm so sorry," she whispered, as the tears continued to run down her cheeks. She could feel her heart breaking bit by bit, just like it had so many times before. This would be the last time though. She knew she would never recover from this.

"Rachel, why would you think I want a Total Power Exchange?" He sounded incredulous, as if he couldn't believe what he was hearing.

"But you said, when you were talking about Karen, that you wanted another slave. And then you kept talking about me wearing your collar and..." She paused and waited for Adam to agree with her, but he just kept staring at her in shock.

"Rachel, that was ages ago. I was joking. Yes, I want you to be my slave, but my sex slave. I love everything about you—your feisty independence, even your stubbornness. Why would I want to change that?" He was serious.

Had she really got it so wrong?

"But…"

"But nothing, Rachel. After all that shit with Karen, I never want another TPE again, but I'll always be a Dom. I'll always need to control you sexually, to restrain you and use you, even inflict pain on you, but only if that's what you want too. What I was trying to say was that I'll never be a nice, normal, vanilla man."

"I never want you to be a nice, normal, vanilla man," she hiccupped. "I love the kink, I wouldn't want you any other way, but I thought…"

"You thought I wanted a twenty-four-seven TPE—all or nothing," he finished for her.

She nodded and quickly wiped another tear from her face.

"Why didn't you say something before?" he asked softly. "If I'd known what you were thinking, I could have reassured you long ago and saved you all this."

"I was afraid you'd leave me if I told you how I felt." Her voice was so quiet, it was barely a whisper. She didn't need him to say anything for her to know exactly what he was thinking—she'd heard it for herself in her own voice.

"This goes back to your trust issues, doesn't it? I thought we'd cleared that up." He took her hand and held onto it tightly while searching her eyes for answers.

"I know, so did I, to be honest. But I was so convinced that you wanted a TPE that it never occurred to me that I might have got it wrong."

"You could have asked me," he said quietly.

"I know. I'm sorry." God, she felt awful. How could she have been so stupid not to trust him enough to just tell him what was bothering her?

Adam reached out and gently wiped another tear from her face then leaned over and kissed her softly on her lips. "This is why openness and honesty are so important in a BDSM relationship. Misunderstandings can easily happen and the consequences can be disastrous. Promise me you'll never keep anything from me again. Ever."

She nodded. "I promise." Did that mean he still wanted her?

"Okay. Then I guess I'd better ask the question I've been meaning to ask all weekend," he said, his eyes radiating love and warmth. "I'd like you to move in with me and to wear my collar permanently. I don't mean as a twenty-four-seven slave, I mean as my submissive and steady girlfriend. Outside the bedroom we'd be equals, but when it comes to sex I'll accept nothing short of your complete and total submission. What do you think?"

Was he serious? "Yes, yes, yes, Sir," she laughed, and threw herself into his arms.

Chapter Nine

Rachel stretched luxuriously and opened her eyes, only to feel a stab of pain behind them. Adam was staring down at her, a soft smile playing on his lips.

It was a week since she'd confronted him at Boundaries, only to find that she had gotten it wrong on a stupendous scale. She shivered slightly as she acknowledged how her stupid insecurities from the past had nearly destroyed their relationship. Thank God he loved her enough to forgive her for her lack of trust. He'd said, right at the beginning, how important trust and honesty were in a D/s relationship, and she had managed to screw it up royally.

And yet, he hadn't dumped her, or punished her by making her feel guilty. Well, at least not after he had given her such a vigorous flogging that had made her scream in...agony? No, more like ecstasy. He'd then made her kneel in front of the whole bloody bar and beg for his forgiveness. Bastard!

Actually, that had sent her into submissive freefall as the humiliation had mixed with the pain of the flogging, and when he'd fucked her shortly afterwards, she had come so hard that she'd thought she would shatter into a million pieces.

"Good morning, gorgeous. Sore head? Better get something for that, you've got a big day today," said Adam, his dimples deepening along with his smile.

Oh, yes. Her stomach lurched with excitement as she remembered it was Saturday. She was moving in with Adam today. He'd given her the day off work yesterday so she and Mandy could pack up the flat. Mandy was leaving for New York after the weekend so the timing had been perfect.

She and Mandy had spent an emotional day packing, cleaning and reminiscing. When they'd finally finished, they'd gone to the pub, drunk nearly a whole bottle of Jack Daniel's between them, and had spent the rest of the evening drunkenly putting the world to rights with the locals.

They'd eventually staggered out of the bar at midnight, where Adam had been waiting to take them home. Rachel had called him at the club during the evening to tell him how much she adored him. It had been an emotional outpouring that had probably been incomprehensible because of her slurred, but heartfelt, words.

Adam, bless him, had been so worried about them walking back on their own, that he'd jumped in his car and waited outside the pub so he could drive them safely back home. On the way, he'd asked Rachel to come back to his place after they'd dropped Mandy off. She had spent the rest of the journey in excited anticipation of what he was going to do to her when they got back, and had then passed out the minute she'd stepped through the door.

She smiled back at Adam and frowned as the pain in her head intensified. "I am never going to drink again," she groaned, as her head thudded with every slow movement.

Adam just laughed. "Serves you right. Come on, up you get. Rob will be here with your things in less than an hour."

Rachel buried her head in the duvet. "Oh, no. Can I Just have another five minutes?"

The next thing she knew, the duvet had been ripped off, and Adam picked her up in his arms and carried her into the bathroom where he unceremoniously dumped her. He marched her to the shower cubicle and turned the water on, eliciting a scream from her as the warm water pounded onto her sleepy body.

"I want you downstairs in fifteen minutes. Do you understand?" he growled.

"Hey," she protested. "You're not my boss now, you know."

Adam just laughed, reached into the cubicle and pinched her nipple. "Fifteen minutes."

Fourteen minutes later, Rachel stepped into the kitchen and felt her heart contract with happiness. The room was lit with bright sunshine streaming in through the open patio doors. Thor and Freya were asleep just outside, looking like two black melting splodges in the hot sun, and the room smelled of bacon and freshly made coffee. A contentedness she hadn't known she was capable of feeling, nearly overwhelmed her as Adam indicated she should sit down at the table, which had been set for breakfast. Next to a glass of freshly squeezed orange juice were two painkillers—he'd thought of everything.

"Take those when you've eaten something," said Adam, as he sat down opposite her. "I want that hangover gone because, apart from the fact that you've got a lot of unpacking to do today, I want you on top form tonight."

Rachel raised her eyebrows. "Why?"

"You'll find out. Now, eat," he said, with a hint of Dom in his voice.

Without even realizing it, she responded with a, "Yes, Sir," and tucked into her toasted bacon sandwich.

Thankfully, the headache cleared quickly and she was ready when Rob pulled up outside in the van he'd hired especially to move her things. Adam had cleared several cupboards and drawers around the house for her, and she thoroughly enjoyed herself as she gradually put her own stamp on her new home.

* * * *

At seven o'clock, they ordered a Chinese take-away and ate it in the garden, enjoying the warm evening sun.

"Luke's opening up tonight, so we don't have to rush," said Adam, as he poured her a glass of lemonade. He'd strictly forbidden her to drink any alcohol tonight and, although she'd been a bit annoyed initially, she was actually quite glad. She wasn't sure how much of last night's drink was still in her system. She knew that BDSM and alcohol didn't go well together, so she guessed that that meant she would be in for an interesting night. Her stomach fluttered at the thought.

Before they left, Adam placed the leather collar around her neck and pulled on the ring to draw her closer to him. He kissed her hard, forcing his tongue roughly into her mouth and taking away her control. She happily relinquished it and melted into his kiss.

When he eventually pulled away, he spoke softly, but firmly, into her ear, "Tonight, you will follow club protocol. I want your complete submission at all times," he growled. "Do you understand?"

A flash of desire blinded her briefly as her breath caught in her throat. Adam reached up and took hold of a fistful of her hair. "I said, do you understand?"

"Yes. Yes, Sir," she gasped, amazed at how quickly she slipped back into submission.

"Any lapse of protocol will be severely dealt with." His voice was hard, telling her the Dom in him was now fully in control.

"Yes, Sir," she whispered, shivering with excitement. Wow, this sounded serious. She couldn't wait.

* * * *

By the time they walked through the doors to Boundaries, with her on a leash, she was already in such a submissive headspace that following protocol came without a second thought. She understood the need for that protocol now. It really did help her to get to where she needed to be.

As they entered the bar, she looked around for her friends. Chrissie was busy chatting to some Doms at the bar, looking ever glamorous in her Marilyn Monroe wig and outfit. Amelia was kneeling, face down, by Jack's feet over near the aftercare lounge. Rachel gulped when she saw his boot holding her head firmly in place on the floor. A few weeks ago she would have been appalled by such a display of complete control, but she knew now how much Amelia loved it. In fact, she understood exactly how her friend would find it such a turn-on, because the thought of Adam doing that to her, actually made her feel quite aroused. Bloody hell, what was happening to her?

Adam led her silently to their table, where Mandy had Dawn on her knees in front of her. This was looking like it was going to be a seriously intense night. The atmosphere was already laced with sexual tension, and her own desire flared as she connected with the ambiance of the club.

She grinned as the heavy sounds of Pain filled the bar—what a great name for a band, and how appropriate for a BDSM club.

Chrissie tottered over with their drinks and joined them for a chat. Well, she joined Adam and Mandy for a chat, because she and Dawn weren't allowed to talk. She felt a small niggle of irritation and quickly quashed it again by winking at Dawn, who looked just as bored as she was.

She sighed as some of her submissiveness slowly drained out of her, only to be replaced with defiance. This Dominance and submission stuff was all well and good, but when her freedom of speech was restricted, she seriously needed to question what the hell she'd gotten herself into. It was the one aspect of D/s that she wasn't entirely comfortable with. And Adam knew it, damn him.

She didn't know what came over her then but, while Adam was discussing some big scandal making headline news, she was overcome by an impulsive moment of rebellion. When Adam wasn't looking, she stuck her tongue out at him, which made Dawn, unsuccessfully, try to stifle a giggle. This only made Rachel giggle back and, suddenly, both she and Dawn exploded into fits of laughter—real, deep in the belly, laughter.

Adam turned and glared down at her. Oh, shit. She knew that look.

"What exactly are you two laughing at?" he said, his voice now a tone deeper and meaner than before.

Unfortunately, this only made Dawn burst into another fit of giggles which immediately re-ignited Rachel's laughter.

"I don't know," spluttered Rachel, and wiped her eyes, which were now streaming with tears.

She tried. She really tried to stop laughing, but the more she tried, the more she laughed, and the more she laughed, the more Dawn laughed. Rachel clutched desperately at her sides to try to ease the cramp from laughing so much, but it didn't help, and she ended up rolling over onto her side with another infectious belly laugh escaping from deep inside her. Dawn, who was taking a sip of water to try to calm down, saw Rachel struggling to control herself and let out a huge guffaw, thus spurting water all over the table. Well, that was it. Rachel was doomed as she shrieked with more uncontrollable laughter.

Adam shot a bemused look at Mandy and they both shrugged, not quite able to believe the sight of the hysterical subs on the floor in front of them. He leaned over and whispered something in Mandy's ear. They both nodded in agreement.

"As you know," said Adam darkly, "I like to make my punishments match the crime, so I think it's time that Mandy and I have a little laugh of our own. What do you think, Mandy?"

"I think that's a mighty fine idea," drawled Mandy, with an evil grin on her face.

Suddenly, all the laughter drained out of Rachel as she was pulled up and marched across the room toward the bar. She glanced over at Dawn as she was also marched to the bar. Adam spoke quietly to Chrissie, who nodded and brought out several plastic wine glasses and filled them with water.

"You haven't done this one in a while," said Chrissie, and laughed when Rachel scowled at her.

Chrissie then took two small round trays and placed four of the full, thin-stemmed, glasses on each.

"Now," said Adam, with a deadly look on his face, "let's see if we can make you laugh again." He turned to Rachel and Dawn and handed them a tray each. "You will each rest a tray on your head and hold it in place with both hands."

He then turned and walked off, leaving Rachel wondering what the hell he was up to now. Then she found out.

"Ladies and gentlemen, can I have your attention for a moment please?"

Uh-oh. The music had been silenced and Adam was speaking over the sound system.

"The two lovely subbies at the bar need a lesson in controlling themselves, so we thought we'd use them as toys in a little game for our amusement. We'd like to invite you to use the feathers on the bar to tickle them. You may tickle any part of their bodies which is exposed."

Thank goodness she was wearing a thong, thought Rachel, and glanced quickly over at Dawn to check what she was wearing. She too, wore a tiny thong which would protect her modesty.

"Their job is to remain still and not spill any of the water they're holding over their heads. After thirty minutes, whichever sub has spilt the most, loses."

Rachel was just wondering what would happen to the loser, when Adam continued.

"The loser gets to spend an hour in the cage suspended over the dance floor."

The cage? No way! The cage was… Well, it was just that—a cage. She'd seen Doms lock their subs in it as punishment—well, she'd assumed it was for punishment. The naked sub would then be hoisted up over the dance floor, high enough that everyone could see them, but not so high as to make them inconspicuous. It seemed like a very public and humiliating penalty for misbehaving, and Rachel had resolved never to risk finding out if that was indeed the case.

She held tightly onto her tray and silently thanked God for her secret weapon. She wasn't ticklish. The only place she might be vulnerable was her pussy but, as that was out of bounds, she'd be fine.

Adam inspected them both, pushing Rachel's legs a little farther apart. She felt open, exposed and, oddly enough, excited. Bring it on.

The first person to have a go was Luke, who had been watching by the bar. "Hold still, sub," he said, and winked at her. He picked up a long feather and slowly ran it down her stomach, sending little ripples of sensation through her body. She shivered slightly, but remained still.

Dawn on the other hand, was already giggling as a Domme tickled her under the arms, and when Rachel heard water splashing on the tray, she knew Dawn wouldn't last long. This was going to be easy.

The next couple of Doms tried their hardest to make her move. One circled the feather around her nipple, which felt delicious, and the other ran it up the inside her right thigh, which made her moan slightly, but still she didn't move.

Dawn was having real problems though. She gave a little squeal as a feather tickled her behind her knee, and, as she struggled to keep her balance, one of the glasses actually toppled over on the tray, sending a spray of water over the poor sub.

Rachel knew she had this in the bag. She hid a smile of smug self-assurance until she glanced back at Dawn, who now looked absolutely mortified, and the smugness drained right out of her. What had she been thinking? It was her fault they were in this predicament. It really wasn't fair to let Dawn suffer the consequences when it had been herself who had started it all by making Dawn laugh in the first place.

She hated the thought of going in that cage, but it had been her stupid defiance that had gotten them in trouble, so it was only right that she should be the one to pay. She swallowed the lump of fear that had formed in her throat, and made her decision.

Her next persecutor picked up the feather and softly tickled her under her chin. At just the right moment, she let out a little giggle. The Dom seemed encouraged by this reaction and teased her neck a little more persistently. Rachel giggled some more before letting out a little squeal. The feather reached round behind her ear and made the delicate skin tingle. The Dom must have thought he'd struck the jackpot when she screamed and dropped the whole tray, sending water cascading across the floor. Well, she couldn't risk Dawn having spilt more than her, so the only way to make sure she lost, was to drop the whole bloody tray.

Dawn stared at her with a mixture of horror, pity and relief. Rachel made sure she looked suitably dismayed and stared, wide-eyed, at the Dom with the feather still in his hand.

The bastard grinned at her and said, "I'll look forward to watching you in the cage later."

She flushed. She knew exactly what he meant. She was only too well aware that she would be completely naked in there, and as she would be suspended in the air the revelers below would get a good eyeful of her private bits through the bars she'd be sitting on.

Adam took her arm firmly and led her away from the bar, a deep frown creasing his brow. When they were out of hearing, he growled, "Why did you do that?"

"Do what?"

Adam took her chin firmly in his hand and glared at her. "You dropped that tray on purpose. Why?"

"Er..."

"If you were so keen to try the cage," he continued, "you could have just asked."

"No. I don't want to go in there," cried Rachel. "I hate the thought of being caged like an animal."

Adam released her chin and crossed his arms. His eyes burned into hers as he studied her. "So, why?"

Damn him. Couldn't she have any secrets without him knowing about them? She scowled and crossed her arms to match his. "Dawn was losing, but I was the one who started it all, and it seemed pretty unfair for Dawn to be punished for something that was my fault."

Adam continued staring at her for a moment, then his face suddenly softened as he smiled. "You old softie," he said affectionately, and drew her into his arms. "That was very honorable of you. Stupid, but honorable."

"I know. I'm sorry about earlier," she said, pulling slightly away and looking up into his face. "I don't know what came over me."

Adam's face clearly showed he wasn't happy, and her heart sank. She'd let him down.

"I asked you to observe protocol tonight, and instead you behaved like an insolent child. I'm disappointed in you, Rachel. I want you to spend the time in the cage thinking about what your submission means to you, and how you've displeased me."

Rachel's face burned with shame. "Yes, Sir. I'm really sorry."

He led her back to the bar, nodded at Dawn and Mandy, then stood back and surveyed Rachel silently. Finally, he spoke, "Remove the thong."

The blood heated in Rachel's cheeks as she looked around the crowded bar. With gritted teeth, she slowly eased the thong down her legs and stepped out of it, leaving her completely naked. The crowd murmured appreciatively and Rachel raised her chin in a vain attempt to show she wasn't bothered.

Without a word, she stepped into the cage and sat down on the cold, hard bars. Adam closed the door and locked it. "Are you all right?" he asked, quietly.

She nodded, not sure what to say at that moment.

"Use your safe word if you panic, or feel unsafe in any way, and I'll get you down straight away. Okay?" His eyes searched hers for any sign that she couldn't cope with this, but she'd be damned if she'd show any weakness, so she stared back, with a small smile to let him know she was fine.

Slowly, the cage was hoisted up and, when it was finally still, she looked down between the bars to find a sea of eyes looking up at her. God, this was so embarrassing. Don't look down, she told herself and fixed her eyes on the fire escape lights instead.

Once she'd gotten used to the height and confinement of the cage, she tried to disassociate herself with the voices below. She tried to think of something pleasant to distract her, but all she could think about was Adam's disappointment in her behavior. She'd blatantly defied his wishes and, not only that, she'd gotten another sub in trouble as well. What had he meant when he'd said he wanted her to spend her time in the cage thinking about her submission? Was he so pissed off with her that he had doubts about their relationship?

She tried to think about it rationally. She knew Adam loved her, and she knew he didn't want her to be more than a sexual submissive, so she was pretty sure their relationship was solid. That helped. It occurred to her then how far she'd come by not assuming he was about to dump her.

But that didn't change the fact that she had displeased him. She felt truly awful about that. Then she realized that he thought she was more concerned by the fact that she was being punished than by the fact that she'd displeased him. But he was wrong, she was gutted that she'd let him down.

She desperately wanted to tell him how sorry she was. She understood now why he had been so angry with her. She'd shown no regard, or respect, for his wishes and had insulted something which was very important to him. He'd specifically asked her to observe protocol tonight, and he wouldn't have done that if he hadn't had a good reason.

She needed to talk to him, to tell him how sorry she was, beg him to forgive her, if necessary, but she had lost all sense of time and had no idea how long she had left in the cage. There was no way she was going to disappoint him even more by asking to come down though, so she remained silent, sitting in her exposed confinement with her guilt punishing her as she knew she deserved.

Suddenly, a voice snapped her back to the present. "Rachel, are you all right?" It was Adam.

"Yes, Sir," she called back.

"I've explained to everyone how you deliberately dropped the tray to save Dawn from the punishment. Everyone seems to agree that you've served your time."

"Oh. Has it already been an hour?"

"No. Twenty minutes," called Adam. "You got time off for good behavior."

She looked down to see if he was joking. The crowd was still there, staring up at her. Then, as if by command, there was a lull in the music — now was a good a time as any, she decided. She wanted everyone to hear her apology. "Adam?" she called, clearly enough for everyone to hear.

"Yes, Rachel?"

"I'm sorry that I disappointed you. You're right, I behaved appallingly and I can only promise never to let you down like that again. I deserve this punishment and will remain here for as long as you feel is necessary."

She watched him take in her words, and saw with relief the smile that spread across his face before he called back.

"Thank you, Rachel, I accept your apology. As far as I'm concerned, you've served your punishment. There's just one thing, though." Adam's voice sounded louder than before, and she realized it was because the music had stopped again. Everyone could hear what he was about to say to her. She just hoped it wasn't too embarrassing.

"What's that, Sir?" she called back.

"Whether I let you down or not, depends very much on your answer to my next question."

What? Now what was he up to?

"What question is that, Sir?" she called, not entirely sure she wanted the whole freaking club to hear whatever it was he was going to make her do.

"Will you marry me?"

A deathly silence fell on the club as every member held their breath. Rachel nearly laughed, thinking he wasn't serious. After all, who could take a proposal of marriage seriously when they were suspended in a cage above a crowd of kinksters? Naked!

"Rachel, I won't let you down until I get the answer I want. It's no longer a question, it's an order — marry me."

Rachel's insides bubbled with happiness as his words finally hit home. Even though Adam had told her he wanted her to live with him, he'd made no mention of marriage before now.

Her heart leaped with joy as she called, "Yes, I'll marry you, Sir. Now will you please let me down so I can show you how much I love you?"

When the cage had been lowered and the door unlocked, Adam helped Rachel out and scooped her into his arms. Before she had a chance to say anything, he kissed her with a fierce possession which nearly took her breath away. Then he reached into his pocket and the crowd let out a huge cheer as he took out a beautiful diamond solitaire ring, which he quickly slipped on her third finger.

"Does this mean we can have an engagement party?" asked Rachel, loudly enough for the crowd to hear. Adam couldn't very well say no in front of the whole club.

"I think that deserves a spanking," said Adam, with a good humored grin.

"You haven't answered her question," called someone from the crowd. "Is she gonna get a party?"

Adam laughed. "Yes, all right, we'll have a party and you're all invited." As the crowd cheered again, he picked her up without another word, slung her over his shoulder and carried her down the steps to the dungeon.

Chapter Ten

Rachel smiled at the pretty, young woman sitting opposite her. "I see you're a teacher. What makes you want to work at Boundaries, even if it is only a temporary position?"

The woman, Victoria, coughed slightly, and replied, "Well, we've just broken up for the six-week summer holiday and, as I'm saving up to buy a house, I thought I'd use the time to earn some extra money."

Rachel nodded, admiring Victoria for having the gumption to take on extra work when others might be tempted to spend the time chilling out on a sun lounger.

Adam had asked her to take over this interview as he'd been called in to the office for an urgent meeting. She'd been nervous at first, but she'd liked Victoria as soon as she had shaken her hand, and soon found she was actually enjoying herself. She already knew she was going to recommend that Adam offer her the job.

"I'll introduce you to Chrissie, the bar manager, in a minute and then she and Mr Stone will make a decision later. Is that okay?"

Victoria nodded eagerly. "Yes, of course." She looked around the empty bar and smiled warmly at Rachel. "I'd love to work here."

Rachel felt herself swell with pride. Even though she didn't own Boundaries, she loved the place dearly. And she loved the owner even more.

She discreetly fingered the stunning solitaire on her ring finger and blushed as she thought back to the day, two weeks ago, when Adam had slipped it on after he'd let her out of the cage. He had taken her down to the dungeon afterwards and given her a deliciously brutal spanking, and had then fucked her hard whilst she'd been tied to a leather swing.

Rachel returned her attention to Victoria and grinned. "So, are you a sub?" she asked. "By the way, your answer doesn't in any way affect the job. I'm just nosy."

Victoria smiled, shyly. "Well yes I am, actually, but I haven't had much experience—or luck."

"Well, I can introduce you to some hot Doms here. In fact, if you like your Doms tall, dark and drop dead gorgeous, then I know just the guy. His name's Luke and he's sexy as hell."

"Rachel?"

Shit! Adam's voice had reverberated through Rachel's body, weakening her knees and sending an instant flush to her cheeks.

"Are you gossiping about the club's members to our prospective employees?"

Rachel saw the glint of humor in his eyes in time to save herself the embarrassment of kneeling at his feet, in front of Victoria, and begging for his forgiveness. Adam had made it clear that, even if they weren't playing, when they were on the premises of the club, she was the sub and he the Dom. Final!

"Yes, I am, Sir," she retorted, bravely and giggled when she heard Victoria gasp. She quickly winked at the girl to let her know she wasn't really in trouble. "Victoria, this is Adam Stone, my fiancé and your future boss."

Adam laughed. "Oh, so you've made the decision for me, have you?"

"I wouldn't dream of interfering," said Rachel, grinning, "but, now that you mention it, you'd be a fool not to hire her."

Adam grinned and playfully swatted Rachel's bottom. "Scoot, you little imp, before I put you over my knee and turn your pretty arse bright red."

"Promises, promises," laughed Rachel, and quickly dove out of his reach. She winked at Victoria and mouthed, "Good luck," before heading back to the office.

She was checking over some accounts, when Adam found her a little while later. Her replacement at work had started last week and, as Joanne Baker was away on business, Rachel wasn't due to start her new job until the following week. In her spare time, she'd helped Adam out with some basic accounting at Boundaries, and even did a bit of waitressing at busy times on club nights, which she'd loved. It had been fine until, on one particular night, she hadn't been available when Adam had demanded his sub back, and Chrissie had put her stilettoed foot down and insisted that Rachel finish the shift she'd agreed to. There weren't many people who dared stand up to Adam Stone, and it had been hilarious seeing him growl something about sending Rachel up to the playrooms the second she was finished.

He'd made her pay later by denying her orgasms, and she'd been ready to murder him until he had brought her to a screaming climax that she was sure the whole bloody club had heard.

She looked up and smiled as he closed the door to the office. "Well?" she asked, leaning back in her chair and crossing her arms. "Are you going to hire Victoria?"

"Do I have much choice?"

"No."

Adam walked around the desk to stand behind her and grabbed her hair, pulling her head gently back so she was looking up into his face.

"For your information, yes I've decided to hire her. Now, I think we need to reset the dynamic here," he growled. The jovial twinkle in his eyes was gone and had been replaced with a dangerous glint, and Rachel's stomach hit the floor when she realized what he meant.

"Whose club are we in?" he growled, tugging her hair gently.

"Yours, Sir," she whispered. Damn him. Why did he have the power to reduce her insides to mush just by pulling her hair and talking dirty to her? Well, other people might not call it dirty talk, but to her, it did exactly what he wanted — brought out her submissiveness and, subsequently, made her horny as hell.

"And who owns who here?" His voice was deep, gruff and sent the little butterflies in her stomach into free fall.

"You own me, Sir," she gasped, through a shiver that shook her to the core. Wow, such powerful words, with such a powerful effect. And he knew it.

"Yes, and don't you forget it. Strip!"

Her eyes widened. "Here? Now?" He had to be joking, surely?

Adam walked around to the front of the desk, sat down on it and indicated for her to come and stand in front of him. "Rachel, I won't say it again."

Oh crap. She hurriedly stood up and made her way around to stand in front of him, glaring daggers at him as she did so. But when she saw his steely eyes glare steadily back, she quickly started to undress until she stood completely naked in front of him. The blood was coursing through her veins, making her slightly giddy. Why the hell was standing naked before a fully clothed Dom so damned sexy?

"On your knees."

Oh, yes. Her stomach fluttered again as she sank to her knees and, when she parted her legs, as she knew he'd expect her to, she was shocked at how quickly she'd become wet.

"Good." Adam stood up and walked slowly around her, inspecting her like a prized possession. "The club will be opening soon and I want you to help Chrissie out until ten o'clock."

That didn't sound so bad. She enjoyed helping Chrissie, although the fact that she would be naked wasn't quite as appealing. At least she wouldn't be the only one, though—nearly half the subs in the club usually ended up naked at some point.

Even with her eyes lowered, she could see his feet walk across the room to a cabinet. It was the cabinet in which he kept his toys. He took something out and returned to stand in front of her. "You are not allowed to come at any time until you're back with me. Do you understand?"

She laughed. As if she would be thinking about orgasms whilst serving drinks to the members. But then she looked up and saw the look in his eyes and her heart sank it dawned on her that he wasn't going to make it quite so easy.

"Get up and bend over the desk," he ordered.

She was about to tell him where to go, but the warning look on his face made her reconsider. She threw him one last challenging glare, then completely contradicted that defiance by bending over the desk, just as he had instructed. She closed her eyes as his rough hand stroked her bottom, and she held her breath with excited anticipation for the first smack she was sure was coming.

Instead of a sexy spanking though, something cold and wet probed the opening to her anus, followed quickly by the same hard pressure she had felt when he'd inserted the butt plug just before the board meeting. She was about to protest, but stopped when she remembered how turned on she'd been. It really wasn't that bad, it was just the slight burn as it went in that was uncomfortable, so she sighed and relaxed her muscles to make it easier for the plug to slip in.

"Good girl." Adam's voice caressed her ears and she moaned softly as the plug seated itself with a little plop. Then, his finger probed her sex and gently stroked her clit. Electricity charged through her, causing her to tighten her muscles around the thing in her arse. Adam removed his finger and chuckled. "I don't think we need any lube here." Before she could comprehend what he meant, he'd filled her pussy with something, not unlike the bullet he'd made her wear on his birthday.

When he was done, Rachel slowly straightened up and gasped as the feeling of fullness asserted itself. It was uncomfortable, but also highly erotic and she couldn't decide whether she wanted to fuck him at that moment, or kill him.

"You will wear these for the whole time you're serving and, I repeat, you do not have permission to come. Is that clear?" Adam's voice had an edge to it that told her he was serious, and Rachel's insides melted a little more.

"Yes, Sir," she whispered, her voice now husky with submissive lust.

He then drew her into his arms and kissed her hard. "When you're done, I'm taking you upstairs and I'm going to fuck you hard."

"Oh... Yes, please."

A few minutes later, as she stood at the bar chatting to Chrissie, the first members started arriving and Rachel started work. She loved chatting to the members, a lot of whom she now knew by name. Serving drinks was a good way to mix with the crowd and she had quickly become popular with both Doms and subs, alike.

She was thoroughly enjoying herself, although the damn high heels Adam had made her wear were killing her feet. Walking gracefully wasn't made any easier by the incredible feeling of fullness, which was always present. But, it could have been worse, so she relaxed and focused on doing her job well. Until a few minutes later. She was successfully balancing a tray full of drinks whilst tottering on her heels, when the plug in her arse suddenly started vibrating, followed immediately by the bullet in her vagina.

How she didn't drop that tray, she'd never know, but somehow she managed to hold onto it as her body went into meltdown. She let out a scream as the shock turned to need, so powerful that her legs actually quivered, and she had to stop and pull them together to try to control herself. That only made her clench tighter around the plug though and she looked helplessly over at Adam as an orgasm started gripping her.

"Oh, fuck," she cried, and grabbed onto the bar to stop herself from falling. Thankfully, just before she was about to give in to the climax, the vibrations stopped and, slowly, her body returned to normal, leaving a dull ache between her legs. "You bastard," she hissed at Adam, knowing she'd regret that later.

By ten o'clock, she'd had another five near misses and spilt more drinks than she had served. Laughing, Adam led her upstairs, tied her to a spanking bench then deftly removed the bullet and plug. She moaned slightly as she was left with a feeling of emptiness that desperately needed to be taken care of.

Then his warm breath tickled her ear as he whispered softly, "Remind me, Rachel. Who's the boss, here at the club?"

"You are, Sir," she hissed, through gritted teeth. "But just you wait till we get out of here. You're so going to pay for this."

Adam laughed. "Hmm... Can't wait. But first, I'm going to have some more fun with you."

He rubbed the soft skin of her ass, leaving a tingling need for more, and when his hand came down on her right buttock with a resounding slap, it didn't take long before the giddiness started to wrap itself around her again. She had already been on the edge of subspace just from her submissive headspace all evening, so it was just a matter of a good, hard spanking to send her deeper into that lovely world where reality felt like fluffy clouds sprinkled with sparkly glitter. All she could remember after that was screaming in a climax so powerful, she thought she'd died and gone to Heaven.

* * * *

It was Friday night and Boundaries would be opening in less than an hour. Rachel sat on a high stool by the bar, waiting for Adam to finish a meeting with the Dungeon Monitors. Chrissie smiled and handed her a bottle of water. "So, sweetie, how's the party planning going?"

Rachel grinned. She and Adam had had so much fun planning the engagement party, discussing who to invite, and who not to invite. They'd finally agreed they would keep the party quiet outside the world of BDSM, and just tell their vanilla friends that they were planning a quiet wedding. Which was true. They just wouldn't mention the collaring ceremony which was planned to take place after the wedding reception.

Adam had been adamant that he wanted a formal collaring ceremony as well as the legal marriage. He'd said the collar was just as important to him as the ring, and Rachel had agreed. She would happily wear his collar knowing he wouldn't be expecting her to submit twenty-four-seven.

"When's the party, again?" asked Victoria, who had been helping Chrissie set up the bar.

"Two weeks on Saturday." Rachel grinned at Victoria and was glad she was working out so well. She had quickly settled into the job, and she and Rachel had become quite friendly in the two weeks since she'd started. The members seemed to like her and Luke had also taken a bit of a shine to her. She knew he'd fall for Victoria's delicate porcelain skin and deep red hair, and Victoria had been just as taken with the tall, dark and gentle Dom.

"You're coming, aren't you, Victoria?" asked Rachel then took a sip of her water.

Victoria's face clouded over for a moment and she looked away. "I'll be there," she said, a little sharply, "but I'll be working."

Rachel frowned as Victoria disappeared across the room and busied herself cleaning the tables in the alcoves.

"Everything all right?" asked Chrissie.

Rachel shrugged. "Yeah, I think so. I really like Victoria, but sometimes I can't work her out. One minute we'll be having a giggle over something and then, suddenly, she'll go all weird."

"What do you mean, 'weird'?" Chrissie looked across the room and watched Victoria working.

"I don't know. It's as if something's bothering her, but she won't say what. I get the feeling she's hiding something, but she won't confide in me." Rachel thought back to the previous day when she'd caught Victoria crying in the Ladies. She'd tried to comfort her and had stayed with her until her tears had stopped, but she had refused to tell Rachel what had been wrong.

"Well," said Chrissie, leaning across the bar, "why don't you invite her out for a coffee after work? Maybe she'd be more inclined to talk away from the club?"

Rachel grinned and raised her hand to Chrissie's for a high five. "That's a brilliant idea. Thanks."

She didn't get another chance to talk to Victoria after that as Adam came back having finished his meeting, and demanded to see his sub in private.

As he closed the door to his office, he ordered her to kneel at his feet then stood, feet slightly apart over her, dominating her space. She lowered her gaze and stared at his boots—big, black and masculine. His leather trousers hugged his legs and she knew that, if she looked up, the bulge from his cock would be large and prominent.

"Look at me, Rachel."

"Yes, Sir." Her voice was already slightly hoarse from the lust snaking itself around her body. She raised her head and met his eyes, which were burning with power and sexual energy.

She knew then what he wanted and her insides flipped as the fire in her belly flared up.

"Suck my cock." He didn't ask, he demanded.

He didn't give her a choice and the heat from her stomach smoldered down to her pussy as she smiled her compliance.

"Yes, Sir." Without another word, she reached for his zipper and pulled it down. The bulge inside sprang out—long, thick and deliciously hard. She quickly undid the button and pulled his trousers down to his knees to free all of him up for her mouth. Then she took his dick in her hands and smiled again, licking her lips suggestively as she rubbed his throbbing cock.

She parted her lips and teased him, leaning forward, but not quite touching it. With a growl, Adam grabbed her head and pushed himself into her mouth. She wobbled slightly on her knees as she struggled to keep her balance, but she wasn't sure if her instability was from the motion or from pure, unadulterated lust.

She took him deep into her throat, cupping his balls in her hands as she did so. Her head spun as he continued to plunge ruthlessly into her, forcing her to take him deeper with each thrust.

She licked, sucked and worshiped his cock, and her own arousal intensified until her clit throbbed so hard that she thought she might come without even touching it. This was one of the aspects of submission that she really loved. Being taken like this, used like an object and yet knowing that she had the power to give him exactly what he needed, in a way that would satisfy him in a spectacular way.

She moaned softly, from need rather than discomfort, and the subtle vibrations from her voice made him thicken slightly in her mouth. The knowledge that she had this effect on him heightened her own pleasure, and she sucked harder and took him deeper still.

Suddenly, he pulled out of her mouth and lifted her up to stand in front of him. Pushing her against the wall, he tugged roughly at her short, leather skirt, exposing her bare pussy to him. With a deep grunt, he pulled her legs up and thrust himself inside her, filling her so completely that it was almost painful. He drove his hips into her, pumping her harder and harder until she felt the telltale thickening inside her, and she heard herself begging him to let her come.

"Come now," he growled, then groaned as he exploded inside her.

"Yes, yes, yes..." She came so hard she thought she might cramp around his cock and never let it go. Now that would be an interesting scenario at the hospital, she thought as the giant waves gradually became little ripples of pleasure.

Still inside her, Adam buried his face in the crook of her shoulder. "I love you," he whispered.

"I love you too. Thank you for... For using me like that. I loved it," she said shyly. Somehow it felt strange admitting to liking something so primal and almost brutal. But she did like it and she knew it was one of the things that made her normal in the unconventional world of kink.

All too soon, Adam sent her back into the club so he could finish what he had been doing before their hot, sexy encounter. She finished her duties with a happy smile plastered on her face then quickly freshened up before the club opened its doors. The bar filled with members, all wanting to catch up with their news before they went up, or down, to play. Adam kept Rachel on a tight leash for most of the night and she didn't get much of a chance to chat with Victoria. She hadn't known her for very long, but she already felt concerned that her new friend had some sort of problem. Chrissie was right. If they could meet up, just the two of them outside the club, maybe Victoria would relax and confide in her.

At around midnight, Adam attached her cuffs to the hooks in the sofa by their table and promised he'd be right back. He was going to take her upstairs for a flogging scene soon and her arse was already tingling in anticipation.

"Hi, there." Victoria smiled as she passed with a tray full of empty glasses.

Great, now was her chance. "Hi. Hey, Victoria." She beckoned for her to come over to her table, and grinned as Victoria quickly glanced over at the bar before sitting down next to her.

"Why has he tied you to the sofa?" asked Victoria, frowning.

Rachel just shrugged. "Oh, he does that all the time. I'm getting used to it. Anyway, do you fancy a quick coffee one day in the week after I finish work?"

To her surprise, Victoria looked horrified. "I…er… I'm sorry. I can't." She jumped up and hurriedly picked the tray up again before disappearing back to the bar without another word.

What the hell was that all about? Rachel stared in disbelief as Victoria fetched another round of drinks from the bar, and carried on serving as if nothing had happened. All she'd done was ask if she'd fancied meeting for a coffee. She couldn't help feeling disappointed. She really liked Victoria and had thought they might become friends, but it seemed she wasn't interested. She sighed and sadly decided that Victoria clearly wasn't the person she'd thought she was.

Chapter Eleven

"Rachel?"

Rachel jumped when she heard Adam's voice beside her. She'd been so pre-occupied thinking about Victoria's strange reaction that she hadn't noticed him sit down next to her.

"You okay?" he asked, pulling her closer to him.

She smiled and put Victoria to the back of her mind. "I'm great. Now will you please release me from this damned seat? I thought you were going to be more relaxed about letting me wander around freely now Karen has gone?"

Adam gave her a stern look, one that warned her not to be so sassy. "I'll decide when I want you restrained. For your information, I tied you to the seat purely because I felt like it. Got a problem with that?" His eyes challenged her, warning her not to mess with him.

"No, Sir," she muttered, and rolled her eyes. "Bloody Doms."

Adam raised his eyebrows. "Pardon?"

Rachel, feeling stupidly brave, stuck her tongue out at him and giggled. "Nothing, Sir." She didn't know why she had these sudden urges to act the brat, but sometimes she just couldn't help herself. She had learnt, though, when she could get away with it and when it would practically be suicidal. Although, of course, she knew she wouldn't really get away with it, but that was where the fun lay.

Adam leaned over and unclipped her cuffs from the hooks in the seat. Without a further word, he snapped her leash back onto her collar and pulled her up to stand next to him.

"I'm going to take you upstairs now and show you what happens to brats who sass their Doms." Although his voice held that sexy, dangerous edge she loved so much, there was also a hint of humor in his eyes — she really, *really* hoped she wouldn't regret her actions.

He marched her to the stairs leading up to the playrooms then stopped and signaled to one of the submissives employed by the club. The girl immediately scurried over to him, head bowed respectfully, and listened intently as Adam said something to her that Rachel couldn't hear. The submissive looked surprised for a moment, but quickly nodded and hurried off to do whatever it was that Adam had asked of her. What was he up to?

Adam tugged on her leash and continued toward the stairs. As he led her into the large, packed playroom, she checked out the flogging rooms — all full. Damn, she had been hoping for a flogging scene. Apart from bare-handed spanking, flogging had quickly become her favorite form of impact play. The trouble was, Adam knew that and so only flogged her as a reward for being a good, obedient little submissive. He also knew exactly what to do to punish her, so acting the brat wasn't as rewarding as it might have been. Still, she couldn't quite quell that little rebellious streak that had always got her into trouble in the past.

Now, as Adam walked her past the spanking benches and flogging rooms, Rachel knew she was going to pay for her cheek. He took her to the back of the long, wide room to where the more intense scenes were carried out. Her stomach fluttered in anticipation when they stopped just outside the room with the enormous bed, but then he turned her to face away from the room. Toward the stocks and pillories.

Her breath hitched as she took in the medieval torture devices. Surely he wouldn't? Her fears were confirmed, though, when he took hold of nape and marched her to the scary wooden contraption. Without a word, he lifted the upper plank and forced her head down onto the middle hole in the lower plank. Before she could even utter her first words of protest, her hands had been placed in the two holes on either side of her head and the top plank lowered again.

The lock clicked as it snapped shut, trapping her like a criminal from the dark ages.

"Adam…" she began.

"Quiet! You don't have permission to speak," he snapped, stopping her mid speech.

"But…" She shut her mouth, aware from bitter experience that he would only make her punishment more severe if she didn't obey him. She wriggled her fingers and tried to narrow one of her hands enough to slip it through the hole, but there was no escape. She was trapped, vulnerable and humiliated, and the realization sent a bolt of lust through her body that was so strong her legs trembled.

Adam chuckled as he knelt behind her. She couldn't turn her head to see what he was up to, but she had a feeling she wouldn't like whatever it was. Sure enough, the zip on her skin-tight micro dress was unzipped and removed, leaving her completely naked. She instinctively closed her legs in a vain attempt at modesty, but Adam had obviously anticipated that and pushed her legs open again.

Then, God help her, he fastened a spreader bar around her ankles, forcing her legs to remain open for all to see. Because the pillory was lower than her own height, she'd had to lean forward to fit into it, which, of course, meant that her bare butt was sticking out, begging for attention. She was well and truly exposed and helpless.

Rachel couldn't decide which she felt more — aroused or mortified. Her heart out-hammered the pulsing throb in her pussy and, when Adam reached between her legs and roughly shoved his fingers into her pussy, she was soaked.

She watched as the submissive who Adam had spoken to downstairs returned with something in her hand. Rachel couldn't quite make out what it was though. Maybe a bottle or something? The girl handed it to Adam, who gave her a curt nod and dismissed her.

Rachel was just getting to grips with being trapped in the pillory with her legs forced open, when Adam cleared his throat.

"Hey, everyone. Look what I've got here." Adam's voice rang clearly through the room during a brief pause in the music.

Bastard, bastard, bastard!

Rachel squeezed her eyes shut as people, not in the middle of a scene, crowded around her and Adam. She could hear their snickers, their hungry, expectant grunts like vultures waiting for their kill. What was Adam going to do?

Then she suddenly felt something smooth and sticky run over her back. Christ, what the hell was he doing? She craned her neck to try to look up, but the damned bar kept her head in place. The thick, gooey liquid spread across her upper back, her shoulders, then the middle of her back and trickled forwards onto to her breasts. It pooled around her hard nipples before falling slowly onto the floor.

She swallowed nervously when the liquid moved lower, over her ass, between her crack and straight to her pussy. When the heat of her vagina mingled with the cool, sticky substance she couldn't stop a groan escaping from her lips.

Then the liquid trickled down her legs, inside her thighs, behind her knees, finally dripping onto her feet. She could tell from the snorts of laughter from the crowd that Adam was thoroughly enjoying her humiliation, and her face heated as she tried to guess what he might do next.

"As you can see, my little subbie has gotten herself into a bit of a mess," he said, laughing. The crowd snickered. Adam ran a finger from her neck, tracing the liquid up over her chin and round her mouth. Then he pushed the finger into her mouth and she finally tasted what it was she was covered in. Chocolate sauce.

"I'd like to invite anyone who enjoys a bit of chocolate to lick my sub clean. You may lick any part of her body which has chocolate on it."

"Any part?" asked a female voice.

"Any. But, no hands."

Rachel's mind went straight to the sticky sauce that had run between her legs. *Fuck!*

"You can go two at a time, for a maximum period of two minutes per person." Adam's words swam through Rachel's mind and her eyes watered at the thought of two people licking her body at once. Two strangers—her stomach somersaulted.

Adam walked round to face Rachel and dangled a blindfold in front of her. "Just to keep you guessing," he said, and covered her eyes with the soft material. When the blindfold was secure, she became aware of his breath on her ear and heard him whisper, "Enjoy!"

A sudden hush seemed to descend around them as someone moved closer to her. Then a warm, wet tongue licked the back of her right shoulder blade. At the same time, another tongue ran up over her left buttock, making her gasp. The tongue on her shoulder then moved slowly, very slowly, around to her front and found the fleshy part of her breasts. It teased her, licking her with little flicks until it reached her nipple.

"Ah!" She cried out as someone took her nipple in their mouth and sucked hard. It hurt but, somehow, she felt the hurt deep inside her pussy and, God, it was good. At the same time, the tongue on her buttock had moved to the inside of her thigh, teasing her, tickling her but never quite reaching the bit that needed it most.

"Time's up." Adam's voice reminded her that it hadn't been him licking her and her pulse quickened.

She heard the rustling of movement then more of the chocolate sauce was poured over her.

"Hey," she cried, indignantly. "That's not fair."

Adam's laugh sent shivers through her. "Who said anything about being fair? My sub. My game. My rules."

The next tongue tickled her softly behind her knees. She shivered as the delicate skin reacted to the stimulation, and she shuddered when a new tongue stroked the soft skin around her belly button.

And so it continued. For what seemed like forever. Adam kept pouring more sauce over her body every time someone new took over and her body became so sensitive that every touch, lick, flick sent little electric shocks straight to her clit.

The fact that her body was available for anyone to have a go at was surprisingly erotic, and Rachel reluctantly admitted to herself that part of the pleasure was not knowing who was licking her body.

The only place no one licked, though, was her pussy. It was the one place that really needed it, but it seemed that Adam had silently made it off limits. Damn! Her whole body was burning with sensation now and the throbbing between her legs was begging for some attention.

Then, finally, someone knelt in front of her, wedged between her legs and the wooden post, and licked some sauce from her bare, smooth mound. *Ooh yes.* Nice. Slowly, the tongue moved down to the top of her slit. It pushed past the hood of her clitoris and gently flicked over her pulsing bud. Her whole body shuddered violently but the tongue moved on, nipping her right labia then the left, before hovering over the entrance to her pussy. It lingered, tasting the chocolate. Tasting her.

She didn't care at that moment whose tongue it was, although she hoped it was Adam's, and she didn't care how many people were watching. In fact, knowing she was on display somehow added to her excitement and she shamelessly tried to buck her hips forward so the tongue would press harder against her.

Then, rough lips nipped her clit and she groaned as the pain heightened her pleasure.

"Please..." she begged. She honestly didn't care who heard her begging for this, all she knew was that she needed to come and she needed it now.

The tongue thrust deeply into her, making her cry out and her inner muscles started to contract around it. Just a little more...

But the tongue pulled out again, leaving her with tears rolling free from under the blindfold. Everyone around them was silent, waiting for her moment and she knew she wouldn't disappoint them. She was so close now.

Teeth nibbled her labia and gently grazed her clit and the burn inside her intensified to the point of being almost unbearable. Then, suddenly, several fingers thrust deeply into her pussy at the same time as the lips clamping hard onto her clit and she screamed as she finally came in a spectacular and glorious grand finale.

As she slowly recovered and the stars in front of her eyes gradually dimmed, she was finally brought back to earth with a brutal bump when the crowd around her started clapping. Adam removed the blindfold so she could see the huge crowd surrounding her. They were all laughing and applauding. At first shame washed over her, but then she saw that their smiles were friendly and their eyes, warm.

How many of them had licked her body? Which ones? Her faces burned as her sticky body shivered in the cool air conditioning.

"Okay, guys. Show's over," said Adam. He swiftly unlocked the padlock and lifted the plank up, finally freeing her. Scooping her into his arms, he carried her over to a sofa and sat down with her on his knees. Someone brought over a blanket and Adam wrapped it around her chilled body. She smiled as she snuggled into his arms and savored his warmth. Wow, that had been intense.

She looked quizzically up into Adam's face. "Was it you?" she asked. She couldn't imagine him letting anyone else get her off like that, but still...

Adam just laughed and kissed her softly. "I guess you'll never know."

Later, as the crowds diminished and the music became quieter, Rachel waited for Adam to finish his brief with the Dungeon Monitors. Adam had insisted on washing her after their scene and she felt cared for and pampered as she waited for him to return. She was sitting on a high stool in the bar, chatting to Chrissie, when Victoria approached her, looking apprehensive.

"Rachel. Could I have a quick word, please?" She sounded shy. Unsure.

"Of course." Rachel smiled warmly and patted the stool next to her.

Chrissie moved discreetly away to the other end of the bar. This should be interesting, she thought as she watched Victoria climb awkwardly onto the stool.

"I want to apologize for the way I acted before. You know, when you invited me out for a coffee." Victoria's hands were clenched as she spoke and Rachel could see she was clearly uncomfortable.

"No worries. Forget it." She smiled to show Victoria there were no hard feelings, but an explanation would have been nice.

Victoria smiled back, shyly, and looked as though she was struggling for something to say.

"So, how are you enjoying the job?" asked Rachel, keen to put Victoria at ease.

"The job?" Victoria's face was blank for a moment before she suddenly forced a smile on her face. "Oh, the job. Yeah, I love it."

"Have you spotted any Doms you like the look of yet?"

Victoria sighed. "It's so much harder than I thought," she quietly. "I just don't know who to trust."

Rachel frowned. Something wasn't right, here. "Victoria. What's wrong?"

Tears welled in Victoria's eyes and she shifted uncomfortably on her stool. "I had a bad experience. Before..." She inhaled deeply and looked at the floor as she spoke. "I was raped."

Rachel gasped and took Victoria's hand. "Oh, Victoria, I'm so sorry. What happened?"

"I'd rather not go into detail, but he claimed he was a Dom and that he would take care of me." Victoria shivered as she recalled her horrific ordeal. "He violated me in every way you could imagine. Ignored my safe word and hurt me in more ways you could know. That's why I came here. I thought it would help me get to know people. You know, who to trust..."

Rachel squeezed Victoria's hand. "I think it's incredibly brave, and clever, of you to get a job at Boundaries so you can move on. Most people would have hidden away and not gone near anything to do with BDSM again."

Victoria's face crumbled though and she whispered, "I'm not brave or clever. Just very stupid and gullible. I'm sorry."

"For what? You don't have to be sorry for anything, Victoria. It's not your fault." Rachel was furious that the poor girl thought that she was in any way to blame for what had happened.

Victoria slipped off the stool, and smiled sadly at Rachel. "You're such a nice person." Then, to Rachel's amazement, she turned and ran off without another word.

How strange. Rachel frowned as Victoria disappeared from view. What the hell was going on? Victoria had just confided something deeply personal to her. That must mean that Victoria considered her a friend. So why had she run off like that? It didn't make sense. And why would she apologize? Maybe she meant that she was sorry for the way she'd reacted over the coffee thing? But Rachel had a feeling that Victoria hadn't told her everything. There was more to this, and Rachel was determined to find out what it was.

"Rachel? Are you ready to leave?"

Adam appeared in front of her and she blinked. She had been so absorbed thinking about Victoria that she hadn't even noticed him approaching. That was definitely not like her. She resolved to have another chat with Victoria as soon as she could and smiled up at Adam.

"Yes, I'm ready." She slid off the stool, waved goodnight to Chrissie and followed Adam out to the car park.

All the way home, Rachel couldn't stop thinking about Victoria, but as soon as Rob pulled up outside Adam's house, a nervous flutter in her stomach reminded her that she had something else to worry about. There was something very important she needed to discuss with Adam. She'd deliberately decided to wait until they got home from the club because she wanted to be on an equal footing with him, and it couldn't wait until morning because she might bottle it by then.

They were greeted by Thor and Freya and she watched silently as Adam fed the two hungry felines.

"Would you like a hot chocolate before bed?" he asked, as he ruffled Freya's fur affectionately.

"Yes, please." She smiled in relief when she saw the Dom in him had gone for the night. She had a feeling he wasn't going to like what she had to say, but with the engagement party only days away, she knew she had to say it now or she may not get another chance.

When the drinks were made, Adam carried them through to the living room and they snuggled up on the sofa. Everything was quiet. Only the ticking of the clock broke the early morning silence.

"Did you enjoy tonight?" he asked, nuzzling her neck.

"Hmm, yes. It was sexy, but I wish you'd tell me for sure that it was you who…you know."

Adam laughed, but didn't reply.

"Er…Adam? There's something I'd like to say before we go to bed." Rachel knew he'd hear the nervous edge to her voice. There was no going back now.

His eyebrows rose slightly and he pulled slightly away so he could look at her properly. "Go on."

She cleared her throat. *Here goes.* "When we get married, I don't want to say the words 'to obey' in the wedding vows." There, she'd said it.

Adam's face remained blank, but his voice was slightly sharp when he replied, "Why?"

Oh, shit. "Well. We agreed that neither of us want a TPE, right? I take my marriage vows to you very seriously and I fully intend to honor them. But, I don't

153

intend to always obey you, because I have my own mind, my own opinions and I'll be damned if I'm going to agree with everything you say if I don't actually agree with you. Don't get me wrong, when you're the Dom—you'll always have my complete obedience and surrender, but as your wife I want us to be equals. End of!" She took a deep breath, relieved that she had finally been able to tell him how she felt. If only she'd done that the first time around.

Adam remained infuriatingly silent and she hoped she hadn't just started a huge argument. She remained equally silent though, deciding that it was up to him to speak first. When he did, she was surprised by the laid-back tone of his voice.

"Rachel. When did I say that I wanted to keep the words 'to obey' in our wedding vows?"

"Well, you haven't, but you must have thought it."

Adam gently took her chin in his hand and held her face so she couldn't look away from him. "Let me remind you. I love you for who you are. I love your stubbornness, your sassiness and your spirit—everything. When it comes to sex, though, I expect nothing short of your complete surrender. Got that?"

"Yes, Sir." Why the hell did she just address him as Sir? Duh!

He grinned, knowing she'd picked up on her Freudian slip. "This is what we'll do. We'll leave the 'to obey' out of the wedding vows, but I want a formal collaring ceremony after the wedding, where you will promise to obey when we're in a D/s setting. I told you I wanted to collar you and I meant it. That is non-negotiable."

God, he was sexy when he was firm. She smiled happily at him, her eyes telling him that she was more than happy with that. "Thank you, Sir."

He grinned. "You seem to have slipped back into sub mode. I think I'll take advantage of that and give you a good, hard spanking for your insolence."

"Yes, please," she sighed, and surrendered herself completely as he pulled her in for a deep, hard kiss.

Chapter Twelve

It was the night of the engagement party and Rachel was as excited as a child going to the funfair. Adam had told her they were leaving home extra early, and she had spent nearly two hours getting ready in anticipation of going somewhere special before the party. She'd tried to guess where they were going, but Adam had been annoyingly coy. Now, she looked at him in surprise as Rob pulled up outside Boundaries. It was only six o'clock and the party wasn't due to start until nine.

"Why are we here so early?" she asked, as they climbed out of the car.

Adam walked around the car, took her chin in his hand and held her gaze firmly as he spoke, "We're on the club premises now, so you no longer have permission to speak freely," he said gruffly.

What the fuck? She stomped after him into the club and couldn't help the frown that she knew gave her discontentment away. This was supposed to be the night of their engagement party. Surely he was going to give her some leeway?

Her frown deepened as he led her into the main bar area, stopped in the middle of the dance floor then ordered her to strip.

"Why?" she challenged, crossing her arms stubbornly.

She barely had a second to think before he took hold of her shoulders and pushed her firmly to the floor. Once she was on her knees, he took a handful of her hair and glared angrily down at her.

"Because we are in the club and I have plans for you tonight. I can easily change those plans, but I'm pretty sure you won't like the alternative version. Now, I'll say it one more time. *Strip!*"

Oh, for fuck sake. Why did he have to be so melodramatic? But she knew he was only putting her into the right headspace for what he had planned, and she also knew he wouldn't have planned anything she wouldn't enjoy, so she grudgingly gave in and started undressing.

"That's better," said Adam gravely. "Because of your insolence though, you will follow me on your hands and knees."

"You mean crawl through the club?" she said, her frown returning with a vengeance.

"No, I mean you should crawl naked through Trafalgar Square. Of course, I mean through the club." He rolled his eyes as if he couldn't believe she'd asked such a stupid question.

But she knew it wasn't the question that was the problem. It was the fact that she had challenged him. Again.

"Sorry," she said sheepishly. "I just need to get my head around the fact that we're at the club so early in the evening." What she meant was, that she couldn't understand why they weren't in some fancy restaurant celebrating their engagement before the party. But she didn't want to sound like a spoiled brat, so she leaned forward onto her hands and dutifully crawled across the dance floor, following Adam as he strode toward the aftercare lounge. The aftercare lounge? But they hadn't even played yet.

Adam pulled the curtain across and Rachel gasped as she finally understood what he was up to. The room was full of flickering candles, creating an intimate and romantic ambiance, and rose petals covered the floor and sofas. Lots and lots of beautiful red rose petals. He picked up a couple of the plump cushions from the sofas, placed them on the floor and nodded at them.

She smiled as she crawled onto the soft cushions. She should never have doubted him. He sat down on the sofa in front of her, bent down and kissed her softly on the lips. "I'm going to blindfold you and restrain your hands, and then I'm going to feed you. I want to show you how special you are to me and how much I treasure you."

She nodded silently and lowered her head in submission. She was finally in that lovely headspace again and would gladly let Adam do anything he wanted to her. He placed a smooth, satin blindfold around her eyes and tied it at the back of her head. Normally, he used a fleece-lined leather blindfold and the difference in the way it felt, surprised her. He then bound her hands behind her back with soft, silk cord, knotting it so she was securely bound without it digging into her skin. He clearly knew what he was doing.

"Wait here, I'll be right back," he said softly, and touched her gently on the head.

She listened to his footsteps walking away from her, toward the bar. She felt the silence that seemed to hang over her whilst she waited alone. Maybe it seemed so much quieter because she couldn't see anything? She was just starting to feel a bit spooked by the intense silence, when Adam's footsteps came toward her again. The curtain pulled open then shut, and a slight breeze brushed against her as Adam sat back down in front of her. Accompanying the rustling of air was a delicious smell of food. She couldn't quite pick out exactly what it was, but her mouth watered at the promise of a treat.

"Take a sip of this," he said and held a glass to her lips. She did as he'd asked and was rewarded with tingling bubbles of fine champagne on her tongue. *Hmm...nice.* She took another sip and giggled when a drop escaped and ran down her chin. Adam's finger gently wiped it away for her.

"Now, I do believe this is one of your favorite foods. Open." Like a bird, she opened her mouth and awaited the offering. *Oh, wow, lobster.* Definitely a favorite. He fed her several pieces of the freshly steamed lobster and she savored every mouthful. Somehow, she was so much more aware of what she was eating than normal—whether it was the fact that she couldn't see the food, or the fact that she was being hand-fed, she couldn't be sure, but it certainly made it taste better.

In between the mouthfuls of lobster, she was given sips of the champagne to wash it down. Hmm, she could get used to this.

"Okay, now on to the main course," said Adam, gently wiping the corners of her mouth for her. "I happen to know that you're rather partial to steak and chips."

If her hands had been free to punch the air, she would have done so. She *loved* steak and chips. Something touched her lips and she opened her mouth eagerly. Ooh, fillet steak, cooked medium rare, just how she liked it. Who had cooked this? There's no way Adam would have had time to cook anything so quickly, so he must have hired a chef or something. And to think she'd been pissed off because he hadn't taken her to a fancy restaurant. This was way better.

"Put this between your teeth and keep it there," he said, as he popped another piece of the tender meat into her mouth.

She did, although it was damned hard not to wolf it down. Then his lips brushed against hers and he snatched the chunk of meat out of her mouth.

"Hey!" She giggled and reached forward in time to bite hold of the meat again and pull it from his lips.

He chuckled and gently nipped her lips. "Greedy."

They didn't talk much—they didn't need to. The intimacy of their shared meal was enough without words getting in the way. In fact, words couldn't express the beautiful closeness, absolute trust and undying devotion she felt at that moment.

Finally, when they'd finished the food, Adam leaned toward her and whispered in her ear, "You'll get your dessert in a minute. I'm going to remove your blindfold and untie your hands now, okay?"

She nodded, still wondering what the dessert might be. As he pulled the satin from her eyes, she blinked slightly and looked around her. The candles were still flickering and the empty plates and champagne glasses were on a tray on the floor.

"Thank you," she whispered. "That had to be the most sensual and enjoyable meal I've ever had."

He smiled and pulled her up into his arms. She snuggled into him, savoring his musky scent and strong arms.

"I love you," he whispered. "Don't ever leave me, will you?"

"Not likely," she replied, with a grin. "I'm afraid you're stuck with me."

"Good." He pulled her closer and held her tightly, as if afraid of letting her go.

"What was that you were saying about dessert?" asked Rachel eventually, and earned a little pinch on her nipple.

Adam grinned, and a hint of something dark flashed across his face. "Oh, yes. You'll get your dessert downstairs. In the dungeon"

The dungeon? Oh, fuck. The last time she'd been down there, she'd called out her safe word.

He then picked her up and carried her across the dance floor and down the steps to the dungeon. It wasn't quite as intimidating without the cries of pain wafting up as they descended the stairs. And the lights were brighter than they had been the last time she'd been there. Being carried in his arms helped too, of course.

Without a word, he strode over to a bench and carefully laid her down on her back. She knew instinctively that he would be expecting her to follow the dungeon protocol, so she remained silent as he strapped her securely to the bench. Silence didn't come easy for Rachel, and it took every bit of her willpower not to demand that he tell her what he was going to do.

When she was completely immobile, he stood for a moment and just looked at her, his eyes telling her she didn't need to worry. The love radiating from them warmed her insides and her heart contracted powerfully in response.

"Rachel," said Adam, his voice gentle. "I want you to experience something new tonight. Have you ever played with wax?"

Wax? Shit! Wax was hot. She shook her head in alarm.

"Don't worry," he soothed. "Wax play can be painful, even harmful, if the player doesn't know what they're doing, but it can also be highly pleasurable and sensual if done properly. I'm going to use a special candle, with no color or perfume, and which has a lower melting point than a standard candle. I promise you won't be burned or blistered. Do you trust me to go ahead?"

She noted that he didn't ask her if she wanted this, but then that was the nature of their play and was one of the things that made it sexy. She liked not being given a choice, not having to think or make decisions. He'd asked if she trusted him to pour hot wax on her and the answer was an unequivocal, yes. She nodded.

"Answer me, Rachel. I need to hear you say it."

"Yes, Sir. I trust you. Completely."

"Remember where we are, Rachel." His voice took on a slightly harder edge and she frowned as she wondered how she'd displeased him.

Oh, yeah. "Sorry. I meant, yes, Master."

He nodded, satisfied, and began gently rubbing something slippery and soothing onto her skin. "This is a natural oil which will make it easier to remove the wax afterwards."

"Yes, Master." She sighed as she relaxed into the sensuous massage and was disappointed when he stopped fairly quickly.

He chuckled softly as if sensing her disappointment, but didn't resume the massage. "If you enjoy this, we'll do it again when we have a little more time. I'd normally melt wax into a vat first, but that takes longer, which is why we're using a candle tonight." He took something out of his pocket and smiled. "I'm going to blindfold you so you can concentrate on the sensations. Don't forget to use your safe word if it's too much."

"Yes, Master," whispered Rachel, and shivered slightly.

"Are you shivering because you're cold, nervous or excited?" His voice was gentle, telling her he wanted to make sure she was completely comfortable with this.

"Er...a bit nervous, Master." Would she ever get used to calling him Master? Technically he wasn't her master, even down here in the dungeon. But actually it did add a rather sexy dynamic to the play, as it left her with no doubt about his power over her.

"Okay. Say 'yellow' if you want me to slow down at any time. It won't end the scene, but it will give you a little respite if it gets too much. If it helps you to know, it's impossible to cause burns with these candles, they're specially made for this. And before I start on you, I'll test it on myself to be absolutely sure it's not too hot." As he spoke, he covered her eyes with the blindfold, throwing her into darkness.

His words soothed her and she relaxed until she heard a match strike. Somehow, hearing that brought the reality back to her. He was going to drip hot wax on her. Fuck!

She gripped the sides of the bench as she braced herself for the heat and was completely caught out by what happened next. Something burned and melted directly onto her right nipple. She screamed in shock, but then realized that it wasn't wax at all. It was ice.

Then something strange landed on her stomach. It was warm, smooth and felt like it had been poured from a distance. It slowly trickled down her sides, tickling her as it solidified and cooled on her skin.

"How was that?" asked Adam.

"Hmm... Nice." She was relaxing now, the fear gone.

He continued to drip the wax across her belly, and slowly her skin became tighter. Only it wasn't her skin, it was wax. The beautiful, warm wax, gently soothing her as it settled onto her body.

She was enjoying it now, and actually looked forward to the next warm kiss of the wax. But, suddenly, instead of warmth, something burned her belly button and she gasped as Adam ran an ice cube over her warm skin. She'd never realized ice was so bloody cold.

She tried to wriggle against the chill until, thankfully, Adam removed the ice. Then it touched her on her lips, melting cool water which ran down her neck. When he finally removed what little was left of the ice cube, her lips were numb with cold. Then, fire kissed them as Adam's hot lips brushed against her own chilled ones.

He continued alternating the hot wax with the ice until, finally, all the ice had melted. At least, that's what she assumed because he concentrated solely on the wax then, which seemed to get closer to her body every time and thereby warmer and more sensuous. She drifted deeper and deeper into the warmth, allowing it to soothe her further. She felt as if she were floating in a tub full of exquisitely warm water — safe, happy.

"Rachel? Wake up, sweet thing."

The words slowly registered in her mind and she opened her eyes to find that the blindfold had been removed. She gazed up into Adam's fuzzy face and tried to work out where the warm bath tub had gone.

Adam leaned down and kissed her lips. "You obviously enjoyed that," he said, with a smile in his voice. "You fell asleep."

She stared at him in dismay. "Oh, Adam. I'm so sorry," she cried, feeling absolutely rotten for falling asleep in the middle of such an intense scene.

"Don't be sorry," said Adam, and gently peeled a layer of wax off her thigh. "I'm glad. It means you enjoyed it."

Something wasn't right, though. When she'd seen the Dom pour wax onto that submissive that first time Adam had brought her down here, she'd clearly been in pain. Enjoyable pain, but pain nonetheless. This hadn't hurt at all.

"It wasn't what I was expecting," she said, with a slight frown. "I thought it was meant to hurt. You know, when we came down here for the first time, that girl was…"

Adam laughed. "First, it's not necessarily meant to hurt. For you, it was meant to be a relaxing and sensual experience. And secondly, Emma is a masochist, so her Dom would have used a wax that had a higher melting point."

Adam continued removing the wax off her body, much to her disappointment. She'd rather enjoyed being wrapped in that warm layer of artificial skin. Now though, as it was slowly stripped away, cool air replaced the warmth, leaving a covering of goosebumps in its wake.

Adam then released her from the restraints and helped her sit up slowly. She felt giddy and slightly disorientated and wanted to lie down again, until Adam wrapped her in a warm blanket and lifted her into his arms. He carried her across the room to a sofa, sat down and just held her.

Party or no party, she would have been happy to have remained there for the whole evening, but eventually Adam broke the spell. "You'd better have a quick shower and get ready. The party starts in half an hour."

"Half an hour? Bloody hell, I thought you were going to fuck me," she wailed in disappointment.

Adam grinned and stroked her hair away from her face. "Later tonight, I'm going to flog that beautiful body till it's glowing, and then I'm going to take you so hard that I won't be expecting you to be able to walk for a while afterwards. Got that?" His words seemed to reach deep into her body, leaving a pulsing need in her pussy that was almost painful.

"Hmm... Yes, Master," she mumbled. "Any chance of you joining me in the shower?"

"Not a chance, you little hussy." He planted a quick kiss on her lips and pushed her gently off his lap.

Laughing, she stuck her tongue out at him and quickly ran off before his hand landed on her arse in retaliation.

* * * *

From then on, the evening had seemed to speed up. By ten o'clock the club was buzzing with music, laughter and screams. Rachel grinned to herself as she surveyed the dance floor. Only a BDSM club could successfully combine friendly laughter with anguished cries of pain.

She and Adam greeted and thanked the well-wishers, some of whom brought gifts, while others tried to find out if Adam intended for his new wife to become his slave. He just laughed and told them that a collar would be involved, but that was as much as he was prepared to say.

As Rachel scanned the room, she made eye-contact with Luke, who grinned at her and blew her a friendly kiss. She smiled warmly back at him, glad he was there. Unfortunately, Dawn had needed to be in New York two weeks ago for her new job, so she and Mandy had been unable to make it. Rachel had had a long and, at times, tearful chat with her old friend on Skype before she'd left for Boundaries earlier, but still, she wished her friend could have been there.

She hadn't invited any of her old vanilla friends, because she didn't think they'd have felt comfortable at the club, although she would definitely invite them to the wedding. At least Amelia was there though. And Chrissie. Victoria was there as well, but she was working. They never had gone for that coffee. Victoria had avoided her after their chat and the poor girl had become more reserved. The feeling that Victoria hadn't told her everything had gotten stronger, but she was no closer to finding out what it might be.

"So, have you set a date for the wedding yet?" a tall Domme, dressed in black latex, asked.

"Not yet," replied Adam, grinning. "But I don't want to leave it too long. I want to make her mine before she changes her mind."

Rachel was just about to add something about keeping him on his toes, when one of the doormen came over and spoke quietly in Adam's ear. Adam nodded and turned to Rachel. "I've just got to sort something out in reception. I'll be right back."

"Don't be too long," said the Domme, "or I might keep her for myself."

Adam laughed and winked at Rachel before disappearing into the crowd. She chatted with the Domme for a while, until Victoria approached with a worried look on her face.

"Rachel? Adam wants to see you in the office straight away." Her voice shook slightly as she spoke, and Rachel wondered what had upset her. Well, if she wasn't prepared to talk to her about it, there wasn't really that much she could do to help.

"Thanks," she said, and felt a surge of excitement ignite in her belly. She excused herself from the Domme, and made her way to the office as quickly as she could. She couldn't help the massive grin that must have been plastered on her face. There was only one reason why Adam would want to see her in the office now, and it wasn't to look at the accounts.

Chapter Thirteen

As Rachel opened the door to the office, she was surprised to see the room looked empty. She smiled as she guessed he must be playing games with her. Was he going to jump out from some hiding place and grab her? Throw her on the desk and maybe ravish her there and then? She giggled as she stepped into the room. "Adam?"

Then the door slammed behind her, and a firm hand grabbed her by the hair and took hold of her arm so tightly that she cried out in pain. Before she realized what was happening, she was forced farther into the room and thrown against the large desk. This wasn't Adam. He would never be so rough with her. As she struggled back onto her feet, a hand slapped her across the face so hard that she fell backwards, and her vision blurred for a second as she tried desperately to work out what the hell was going on.

In that split second though, her attacker had clipped metal handcuffs around her wrists then deftly attached them to a chain that had been locked around the leg of the solid, oak desk. As her vision slowly cleared, the image of Dominique's twisted face gradually materialized in front of her, and her heart sank as she acknowledged that she was in very real danger.

"Karen, for God's sake," she cried, "let me go." She knew her words were futile, but she didn't know what else to say. Suddenly, the same fear she'd felt the night Karen had attacked her in the club gripped her heart so tightly, she had to gasp for breath.

"Don't you dare call me that, you fucking whore," snapped Karen, and threw a heavy punch against Rachel's right cheek. Fiery pain brought flashes of white light across her eyes and she tried, in vain, to bring her hand up to protect her face.

"What do you want?" gasped Rachel through the throbbing pain of her cheek.

"I want you dead," growled Karen, as she reached for something behind the desk. "And, once you're out of the way, I'm going to get Adam back."

Something changed in Rachel's fear then. It was as if it hardened into a ball of rock, with fire trapped inside. As the pressure built, the rock exploded like a volcano and the fear turned into angry molten lava, seeping out of her pores with a need for survival, so strong, that nothing would stop it.

"Karen, when will you get it through your thick head that Adam doesn't want you? Whether I'm here or not, he will *never* take you back." Her anger simmered dangerously under the surface, ready to explode if Karen touched her again. If her hands were free now, she'd knock her bloody lights out.

"Of course he will. He loves me," said Karen in a strangely calm voice. "He may think he doesn't right now, but that's because you've poisoned his mind. Once you're gone, he'll realize that it's me he wants."

"You poor, deluded little woman," spat Rachel. If it wasn't for the fact that she was in serious danger here, she might almost feel sorry for Karen.

"We'll see." Karen picked a can up and started pouring some sort of liquid in a large circle around the desk, stopping by the door. As Karen put the can down on the floor next to her, Rachel finally smelled what the liquid was. Shit! It was petrol.

She tugged at the chain securing her to the desk and wondered how much strength it would take to lift the thick, heavy leg of the solid desk. But she knew it would be impossible, that desk was so heavy she could barely push it, let alone lift a leg up with cuffed hands.

"Karen...Dominique, let's talk about this," she cried, desperate to buy some time.

But Karen ignored her and reached into her pocket, quickly pulling out a lighter which she held up for Rachel to see. "Goodbye, bitch," she growled, and flicked the lighter on.

Panic tore through Rachel then, as she realized that Karen was deadly serious. She closed her eyes and waited, with sickening dread, for the heat of the inevitable flames to engulf her. But instead, she heard the door crash open and Adam calling her name.

"Rachel!" He froze when he saw her chained to the desk and surrounded by a wet trail of petrol.

As if in a movie, Karen stepped out in front of him, holding the lighter dramatically up in front of his face.

"Karen," he growled. "What the hell do you think you're doing? Give me that lighter. *Now!*"

Karen just laughed and waved the lighter farther out of his reach, taunting him. "I'm getting rid of her for you," she cried. The madness in her voice was clear.

"Then we can go back to the way we were before *she* came along and ruined it all."

Adam glanced over at Rachel quickly and, somehow, in that split second, sent her a silent message to remain strong.

He turned back to Karen and softened his voice. "Karen. You and I were finished a long time before Rachel came along. You must accept that we'll never get back together again. It's over."

Rachel held her breath as she waited for Karen's response. But, she couldn't believe her eyes when it came, as Karen suddenly threw herself onto her knees in front of Adam, in what she recognized as the slave position. "Master. I beg you to take me back. I'll serve you in any way you require, and I'll be your loving and faithful slave for as long as I live." Her voice had become desperate, and along with that desperation— Rachel knew that Karen had become more dangerous.

Adam stared at Karen in disbelief. "For God's sake, Karen. Get up!"

"But I love you, Master," she wailed, almost hysterically.

"No, you don't," said Adam coldly. "You never loved me."

Karen looked up into Adam's face, and finally appeared to see the contempt in his eyes. Her body stiffened, the submissiveness visibly draining away, leaving it trembling with rage.

"Noooo," Karen screamed, and quickly scrambled back to her feet. Her eyes had a new look of madness in them, a look that was far more terrifying than anything Rachel had seen before now. She watched in horror as Karen suddenly picked up the petrol can and doused herself in the pungent liquid. When Karen had dropped to the floor a moment ago, Rachel had noticed that she'd dropped the lighter, but she had somehow managed to pick it up again as she'd stood back up, because she now waved it scarily in the air with renewed fervor.

"If I can't have you, then neither will she," she growled, her eyes flashing with fury. "She's surrounded with the petrol, Adam, so if I go up in flames, then so does she."

Adam didn't have a chance to react because Karen flicked the lighter on and held the flame up in front of his face. There was nothing he could do. Rachel guessed that he might be trying to work out if he could get to her in time if the room went up in flames, but, even if he did manage to reach her, she was handcuffed to the desk and he didn't have a key. He wouldn't be able to save her.

Maybe Karen was just stalling for time. Maybe Adam should tell her what she wanted to hear and she'd give him the lighter? But Rachel knew that, even if Adam did play along, there was no way Karen was going to let her go.

Then her worst fears were confirmed when Karen let out a spine-chilling scream and the room lit up with the whoosh of a flame igniting. She wasn't sure if Karen really had intended to set herself on fire. Had she waved the lighter in the air just to scare Adam? Whatever Karen's intentions, the flame must have caught the petrol because, suddenly, the room was alight.

Rachel could no longer see Adam or Karen through the flames surrounding her. They had taken hold so quickly that she hadn't had a chance to see what had actually happened. All she could see now was smoke—thick black smoke and it was creeping closer toward her.

Her eyes stung, her nose stung and her lungs stung. She could no longer see anything for the smoke, and she knew she didn't have very long before she succumbed completely. Was this really how she was going to die? She thought of Adam, and her heart broke for him. Would he ever get over this?

The strength drained out of her. She couldn't breathe. Every time she coughed, she just inhaled more of the thick, acrid smoke until she felt as though her whole body was consumed with it. Her eyes closed and she waited for the final breath to leave her body. At least she would die before the flames reached her. Her last thought before the blackness enveloped her was of Adam, and how her love for him would never die along with her. She just wished she could have told him that.

* * * *

Rachel opened her eyes and quickly closed them again. Was this Heaven? It must be because she just saw Adam's pale, drawn face smiling down at her.

"Rachel?"

Yep, that was definitely his voice. Hang on, why was he in Heaven with her? He hadn't died, had he?

She opened her eyes again and, sure enough, there he was. But her eyes hurt. She needed to shut them again. But if she did, she might lose him. As her lids grew heavy again, she heard his voice, excited, panicky, desperate. "Nurse! Nurse, she's awake. She opened her eyes."

Then it all went black again as she drifted in and out of the strange fog which seemed to surround her.

When she opened her eyes again, she found herself looking up into the face of a woman.

She smiled efficiently as she spoke. "Hello, Rachel. Welcome back, I'm Doctor Richards. You gave us all quite a scare."

"Adam?" she croaked. Why wasn't her voice working? Where was Adam?

"I'm right here, Rachel," called Adam from behind the doctor.

"Mr Stone, kindly step back while I see to Miss Porter," said the doctor firmly. Despite everything, Rachel smiled at hearing Adam being told what to do.

When the doctor had checked her over and finally left the room, Adam took her hand and smiled down at her. "I was so worried," he said, his voice breaking slightly as he tried to hide his anguish. "Thank God, you're all right."

"What happened?" she croaked. Her head was foggy. For some reason, she couldn't quite reach the part of her brain that held her memories.

"You were in a fire," said Adam softly. "But you're safe now."

Oh, yes. It was coming back now. "Dominique..." she cried.

"Karen is dead. She won't hurt you again."

Dead? So it hadn't all just been a horrible nightmare. "I'm sorry," she whispered.

"Hmm...I'm not sure I am. She tried to kill you. I thought I was too late," he whispered. "I thought I'd lost you." His voice shook as he spoke and tears pooled in his eyes.

"How did you get me out?" She remembered the handcuffs that had prevented her escape. There's no way Karen would have given him the key, so how did he get them off?

"I cut the cuffs off you. All the Dungeon Monitors in the club, including myself, carry strong metal cutters as a safety precaution," he replied, reaching out and taking hold of her hand.

It felt strange. She glanced down and saw that it was covered in bandages.

"Your hand..." she gasped.

"It's only a little burn. It's fine. I grabbed a blanket, and covered myself as I ran into the flames to get you. Once I'd cut you free, I wrapped you in the blanket and got you out just as the flames closed in. My hand must have got in the way," he said, with a wry smile.

"You could have died." She closed her eyes again and a tear escaped from beneath a lid. He'd nearly died because of her. He'd saved her.

"Rachel, there's no way I was going to let you die in there. I'd rather have died myself."

The emotion in his voice brought more tears and her throat contracted painfully as she tried to stop herself from choking on them.

"I want to go home." She desperately needed to get away from the hostile environment of the hospital, and be home in the safe comfort of Adam's house — their house. She wanted to watch Adam prepare dinner in the kitchen, while Thor and Freya slept in a sunny corner of the garden. She wanted to put the fire behind her and forget about it. As if it had never happened.

"I know, but you'll need to stay in hospital for another day, because of the smoke inhalation. They want to keep an eye on your lungs."

She tried to feel the pain of burns, but her body felt numb. "Am I... Am I badly scarred?" she whispered.

Adam shook his head. "You have a nasty burn on your left arm, which might leave a scar, but that will fade in time. You were lucky, another minute and..."

His voice broke as he struggled to regain some control.

"Adam, I thought I was going to die." Her croaky voice was now barely a whisper.

A tear ran down Adam's face as bent his head to her chest. "Oh, Rachel. I'm so sorry."

"It's not your fault. You saved me."

"Karen was my problem, not yours. I should have realized that she wouldn't let go so easily."

"You weren't to know. How did you know where to find me?" She had a vague memory of getting some sort of message.

"Victoria told me. She literally dragged me back through the club to find you."

Oh, yes. She remembered now. "But it was Victoria who gave me the message to meet you in the office." That didn't make sense. Why would Victoria have given her a message that would have lured her into danger?

Adam looked uncomfortable, and she immediately saw the hesitation in his eyes.

"What?" she demanded. "What aren't you telling me?"

He cleared his throat and spoke slowly. "Victoria was working for Karen. She had been instructed to let Karen in through the back door then get you to the office alone. Karen had told her that she wouldn't actually harm you, but, after she'd given you the message to meet me, she followed you and listened at the door. She went straight to reception to find me as soon as she realized what Karen was up to." Adam took her hand and gently stroked it, as if trying to soothe away the painful words.

Rachel closed her eyes. This was all too much to take in. The enormity of Victoria's deception hurt and she felt a flash of anger as she recalled how she'd tried to befriend and help her.

As if reading her thoughts, Adam said, "Don't be too hard on Victoria. If she hadn't come to get me as soon as she'd realized what Karen was going to do, I probably wouldn't have got to you in time."

The thought was a sobering one.

"The club," she cried suddenly, as visions of the flames suddenly flared in front of her eyes. "What happened to the club and everyone in it?"

"It's fine. The fire fighters arrived in time to get everyone out, and they managed to contain it to the office and surrounding corridor. The office is destroyed, but we can easily rebuild it." He gently stroked her forehead as he spoke. "You should rest now," he said, the deep, velvet tone of his voice comforting her. "I want you recovered as quickly as possible, because I have plans for you, Rachel Porter."

"Hmm... Yes, please," she murmured, feeling a ridiculously strong rush of happiness wash over her. Despite the fact that she had nearly died last night, and that Karen did actually die, she felt a deep sense of well-being that she couldn't quite understand. She reached out for Adam's hand as her eyes grew heavy again. He took it and gave it a gentle squeeze. He didn't need to say anything for her to understand the depths of his emotions. She just knew, as if they were connected somehow.

She recognized the feeling now. It was Adam's total devotion to her, and her alone, that gave her that warm glow of contentment. She knew he'd never left her bedside since she'd been brought to the hospital, and she also knew that he would be just as lost without her, as she would be without him. They belonged together. In fact, they were soulmates.

Soulmates with kinky needs that complemented the other's perfectly.

She must have drifted off to sleep because, when she opened her eyes again, Adam had been replaced with Victoria. It took a moment to remember why she wasn't too pleased to see her, then it all came back to her.

"Get out," she growled. Anger simmered deep inside her as she remembered Victoria's betrayal.

Victoria looked distressed, though, and wiped a tear from her eye. In fact, she looked awful—deep lines were etched across her face, showing the stress she must have been under, and dark shadows under her eyes made her look haunted.

"Please, hear me out, Rachel. Let me explain and then, if you still want me to leave, I will. I promise." Her voice trembled, and sounded defeated before she'd even had the chance to speak.

Rachel didn't say anything. She didn't have the strength, so she just nodded her head to let Victoria know she could stay.

"Thank you," whispered Victoria. She waited to see if Rachel was going to say anything and, when she remained silent, Victoria continued, "Well, I'd had fantasies about being dominated for years, but had never done anything about it. I was having dreams about being tied up and spanked by a strict, sexy Dom and it got to the point where I felt I had to do something about it."

Rachel grudgingly understood exactly what Victoria meant. It wasn't that long since she'd been there herself.

"I decided to go to a fetish club in Soho to see what it was all about," continued Victoria. "I didn't know what to expect—I was absolutely terrified, but I knew it was something I had to do. Well, I met a guy there, Mitch his name was, and he seemed really nice. He said he could tell I was a newbie and offered to Top me to see if I liked it. I stupidly agreed and went back to his place." She sighed, and checked to see if Rachel was still listening. She was.

"When we got there, he offered me a drink and that's about all I remember. He'd drugged me and..." Victoria choked slightly on her words as she continued, "and he raped me while a woman took photographs. When I woke up, the woman, Dominique, showed me the photos, which made me look like a dirty tart. You certainly couldn't tell it wasn't consensual. Dominique told me that if I didn't agree to do what she said, she'd send the photos to the head teacher at my school, and tell him I was a BDSM whore."

Despite Rachel's resolve not to believe any of Victoria's story, she felt a pang of sympathy as tears filled the girl's eyes. Retelling the story couldn't be easy and Rachel reached out for her hand to help her finish it. Victoria took her hand gratefully and smiled sadly.

"Dominique told me she wanted me to get a summer job at Boundaries and all I had to do was tell her what the plans for your engagement party were. She wanted to know dates, times, stuff like that. Then she said the only other thing I had to do was to let her in through the back door on the night of the party, and get you to go to the office alone at a given time."

Victoria held tightly onto Rachel's hand as she cried, "She promised she wouldn't hurt you, Rachel."

"Well," said Rachel, her voice still husky from the smoke, "that explains why I had the feeling you were hiding something."

Victoria nodded. "Yes, I'm sorry about that. I really liked you and felt we could be friends, and then I'd remember what I had to do and feel so bloody guilty that I couldn't face you. When you invited me out for that coffee, I was gutted because I really wanted to go. I just couldn't bring myself to lie to you. I'm sorry."

Rachel smiled. "Adam tells me that it's because of you that he got to me in time. It seems I owe you my life."

"It wasn't until I heard Dominique threaten you in the office that I realized what she was going to do. I'm so sorry."

Rachel's heart went out to Victoria. What the poor girl must have gone through. And here she was, explaining it all to her. She didn't have to do that.

"What happened to the guy who raped you?" she asked, deciding that if he wasn't already in jail, then she'd personally see to it that they caught him and threw away the key.

"His job was to create a diversion in reception. The plan was to get Adam away from you so I could give you the message to get you to the office. When I saw him in reception though, I freaked out and told Luke what he'd done. Luke grabbed him and called the police. Luke told me later that he thinks he might have broken Mitch's arm when he struggled."

"Good," growled Rachel. She'd break more than his arm if she got hold of him—he certainly wouldn't be capable of raping anyone again.

Victoria stood up and looked at Rachel with eyes leaden with guilt and remorse. "I'll go now," she said quietly. "I just wanted to explain and say how sorry I am."

"Wait." Rachel reached out her hand and took hold of Victoria's arm. "Don't go."

Victoria looked like she didn't quite know what to do. "Are you sure?" she asked, hovering uncertainly by Rachel's bed.

"Yes, please stay. I don't blame you, Victoria. How about we go for that coffee as soon as I'm out of here?"

Victoria's face broke into a huge smile and the stress on her face drained away. "I'd love that," she said, and sat back down next to Rachel.

Victoria stayed for another five minutes before being shooed out by the nurse. After mulling over their conversation she fell into a deep sleep, and when she woke, Adam had returned. She told him about her visit and how Victoria had agreed to help her with the wedding plans. Adam smiled and, in typical Dom fashion, ordered her to be quiet so she could rest her throat.

She closed her eyes, finally giving in to her exhaustion, and listened happily to Adam talking about their wedding arrangements, and all the deliciously naughty things he was going to do to her once she was better. The last thing she heard before she drifted off to sleep was Adam saying something about a collar that he was going to place around her neck on the night of their wedding.

Chapter Fourteen

Rachel looked around the huge room, filled with flowers, balloons and smiling, happy people toasting them with the finest champagne.

They say that a girl's wedding day is the happiest day of her life, but nobody could truly understand the real truth behind those words until it happened to them. She felt as if the day was passing in a blur, like it was slipping by whilst she was watching from inside a bubble. It was all happening too quickly, and she wished she could turn a dial to slow things down a bit. Well, maybe not too much, because after the reception, they were off to Boundaries for a different kind of ceremony.

The catering staff cleared the remaining dishes away and refilled the glasses with champagne. The food had been amazing, although she'd been too excited to eat any of it. Adam had made her eat the seafood starter though, saying that she would need her strength later. Her body had sizzled at the thought, and she had quickly wolfed the food down, although she'd hardly tasted it.

Everything about today had been perfect. She had felt like a princess as she'd walked down the aisle in her beautiful, simple ivory silk dress. Luke had given her away and Chrissie had been Adam's best man. She nearly hadn't recognized him in his smart top hat and tails.

She grinned as she thought back to the vows they'd taken in front of everyone earlier. At least half the crowd had snickered quietly when the words 'to obey' had been left out. She was so glad she'd made her feelings about that clear from the beginning, and that Adam had agreed. She was also deeply touched and honored that he wanted a collaring ceremony in addition to the wedding. It was the perfect balance. As his wife, she would be his equal, but as his submissive she was more than happy to promise to love and obey.

Mandy and Dawn were there, having flown over from New York. Mandy was her bridesmaid and had helped Rachel get ready that morning. They'd had an emotional talk the night before, where they'd both vowed to be best friends forever, whatever happened and wherever they were in the world. Their champagne fueled talk had quickly turned to smut, and they'd giggled their way to sleep at four o'clock in the morning.

Mandy and Dawn weren't the only ones who'd traveled to attend the wedding. Adam's parents, whom she'd only met once before, had flown over from Spain, where they lived in happy retirement. They were lovely people, warm and friendly, and had been genuinely happy for Adam that he had finally found his perfect bride. His mother, Susan, had knocked on Rachel's door while she'd been getting ready earlier and had given her a sapphire ring.

"It was given to me by Adam's grandmother on our wedding day, and I want you to have it." She'd had joyous tears in her eyes, and had returned Rachel's hug warmly when she'd thanked her.

Someone touched her arm, and she looked around to find Joanne Baker smiling at her.

"Thank you so much for coming, Joanne," said Rachel, smiling warmly at her new boss.

"I wouldn't have missed it for the world. It's thanks to you that Adam is so much easier to work with these days." She winked at Rachel, who giggled.

She loved her new job and was quickly getting to grips with the basics of accounting. She was due to start a part-time course at college in September, which would give her the formal qualifications to advance in her new career. Joanne had been very supportive and the whole staff had welcomed her to the team. Joanne gave her a hug and returned to her table where Rachel's new colleagues were finishing their dessert. Joe and her old team were there as well and had all been truly happy for her. The looks on their faces when she'd told them she was going to marry the boss had been priceless. Joe had hugged her and wished her well and the girls had all wanted to know how she'd tamed the formidable Adam Stone.

She scanned the room looking for Adam and when she spotted him a rush of love flooded her body. He was laughing with some friends from university, and her heartbeat quickened at the sight of him. As if sensing her eyes on him, he turned and smiled. That smile could have been proof of synchronicity. They could have been millions of light years apart and would still have had that special connection.

He excused himself from his friends and returned to her, pulling her into his arms as if the five minutes they'd been apart had been an eternity.

"Are you okay?" he murmured, nuzzling her ear.

"I'm more than okay," she replied, happily. "I've never been happier in my life. It's been such a perfect day, hasn't it?"

He nodded and kissed her softly on her lips. "Yes, it has and we're only halfway through. Are you ready to wear my collar?"

She laughed. "It's a bit late asking me now."

Adam raised an eyebrow, and she got the message with an excited thud in her stomach.

"Yes, Master. I'm ready."

"Good. Let's start saying our goodbyes. Rob will be waiting outside and our kinky friends will meet us at Boundaries in an hour. Do you remember what to do when we get there?"

Rachel nodded. "Amelia and Victoria will take me to the office to get ready. They'll then lead me through the club to where you'll be waiting."

"Good." He kissed her again and took her hand as they started saying their farewells.

* * * *

Rachel's stomach was turning Olympic sized somersaults by the time they arrived at Boundaries. For some reason she was more nervous now than she had been before the marriage ceremony that afternoon.

Amelia and Victoria had left the reception a few minutes before she and Adam had, and they were now waiting by the entrance to the club. They smiled as Adam handed her over to them, and led her silently to the office where she was to be prepared for the ceremony.

The office was finished now, finally. It had taken months to rebuild, but now it looked beautiful with its new furniture and fully equipped toy cupboard. There was a small, private room to the side of the office which housed a comfy living space, with soft, squidgy sofas and, coming off that, there was a small but perfectly equipped bathroom. Adam had actually put hooks in the shower cubicle, but she had yet to find out what he intended to use them for. As if she didn't know.

Amelia and Victoria removed her dress and stripped her naked. They then led her into the shower cubicle, where they washed her. Rachel didn't need to do anything, and she smiled as the women's hands softly massaged her body. Even though it wasn't sexual, there was something sensual about being washed by two women, and Rachel relaxed and allowed herself to enjoy the experience of being pampered.

When she had been washed, shaved, exfoliated and moisturized, Amelia and Victoria dressed her in a white, see-through gown, leaving her completely naked beneath. She would be barefoot, with no makeup, perfume or jewelry. The only thing she would be wearing, apart from the flimsy scrap of material on her body, was a crown of thorns on her head.

Finally, she was ready. Amelia kissed her lightly on the lips, and Victoria gave her a warm hug, before opening the door and leading her out.

Rachel's stomach tightened as she heard the low murmur of voices in the main bar, and her legs trembled as she put one foot in front of the other. This was way scarier than walking down the aisle of a church.

She turned to Amelia on her left and whispered in her ear, "Why do I feel like I'm a sacrificial lamb being led to the altar?"

Amelia grinned and replied, "Because you are, my dear."

"Thanks," she muttered under her breath, and tried to steady herself as they got closer to the hum of voices.

When she was eventually led into the huge bar area, she was astounded by how many people there were, all standing in a semi-circle with a large space in the middle. *Oh, God!* She somehow hadn't been expecting such a big crowd, and her stomach twisted with nerves as Amelia and Victoria paraded her around in front of the crowd, displaying her for all to see.

Then they led her over to where Adam was standing and her heart literally jumped into her mouth. Suddenly the nerves vanished as she felt she'd come home—to her Master.

Amelia and Victoria pushed her gently onto her knees in front of him and she bowed her head as she knelt by his feet. She couldn't see what was going on around her, but she heard footsteps approach and stop next to Adam.

Then she heard Luke's voice. "Ladies and gentlemen, Masters, Doms, Dommes, subs and slaves. Have I forgotten anyone?"

There was hushed laughter from the crowd before Luke continued, "I'd like to welcome you to this very special occasion where Adam Stone will collar his new wife in front of everybody here. As you all know, the meaning of the collar varies according to different people, but the one thing that never changes is the fact that the collar is a symbol of absolute love, trust and ownership.

"It's an honor for any submissive to wear her Master's collar, but it's just as much an honor for that Master to have earned enough trust and respect from their submissive, that they agree to wear that collar.

"Adam and Rachel do not have a twenty-four-seven Master/slave relationship and have therefore decided not to be too formal tonight. There will be no rituals, no blood or hand tying. But there will be promises made which are just as heartfelt and binding as those of any other collaring ceremony."

The crowd remained completely silent when Luke stopped talking and Rachel's heart pounded so loudly that she was sure everyone could hear it.

Then she heard Adam's voice. "Rachel, you may look up now."

As she looked up at his face, all the nervous energy that had been torturing Rachel a moment ago, turned into glorious submissiveness, and she hoped that Adam could see it in her eyes. He smiled down at her and she knew that he did see it.

"I just want to say how lucky I am to have found this beautiful lady, who has not only become my wife, but has agreed to wear my collar as my permanent submissive." His voice was deep, velvety and tinged with undisguised emotion. "I feel truly honored by her gift of submission and promise to always treasure and nurture it."

Amelia approached then, carrying the collar, which Rachel hadn't seen yet. As Amelia handed it to Adam, Rachel gasped when she finally saw it. It was a replica of the collar on the picture he'd drawn of her, which now had pride of place in their bedroom. The silver, choker-style necklace was encrusted with tiny diamonds, and was simple and elegant. Her eyes filled with tears as she looked at it and Adam smiled, understanding her emotion.

"Rachel, I promise that I will always love you and treasure you as both my wife and my submissive. I will always strive to be worthy of your love and submission, and will look after you and protect you. Your needs will always be my main concern, and I promise to respect and meet those needs as best I can. I am deeply honored by your complete trust in me and I promise never to betray that trust. This collar is a symbol of my love and ownership of you. Although we have agreed that this ownership does not involve a twenty-four-seven Total Power Exchange, it does mean that, even when we're not actively playing, you are mine in mind, body and spirit. Rachel, do you accept this collar as a symbol of my ownership of you?"

Rachel was so moved by his words that she struggled to reply. "Yes, Master. I do," she said, hoping her voice was audible.

Adam smiled, leaned down and placed the collar around her neck, snapping it shut at the back with a small padlock. Her head was swimming with happiness, and it took a few moments before she remembered that it was her turn to say something. Her throat tightened with nerves, and she prayed she wouldn't forget her words. She wanted them to be perfect, just like Adam's had been.

She cleared her throat. "By accepting this collar I promise to be your loving submissive. I promise that I will wear the collar with pride and that it will symbolize my submission to you at the times we have agreed. During this time, I promise to serve you, honor you and obey you, but, even outside these times, my love and respect for you will always be reflected in it. I happily and willingly kneel to you as a sign of my love and devotion."

As she spoke she looked only at Adam's face and was moved to see tears in his eyes. He quickly pushed them back before anyone else saw the raw emotion. It was meant for Rachel's eyes only.

Suddenly the crowd let out a huge cheer that filled the room with its genuine good wishes. They clapped and whistled, and it took quite a while before they quietened down again.

Finally, Luke held up his hand and the room became quiet again. Then he started to speak. "As you know, Adam and Rachel have decided to forsake the more traditional Ceremony of Roses because they don't live the lifestyle twenty-four-seven. But, Rachel's collar is just as important to them as her wedding ring is, and they would like to mark that. On the table to my right, are two large glass bowls, one filled with white rose petals and one filled with red. The white petals symbolize Rachel's pure and beautiful gift of submission to Adam. The red petals symbolize the passion and protection of his dominance of her. Please take a handful of each and throw them at the couple to celebrate their merging."

Adam took Rachel's hand and helped to her stand up. As she did so, they were showered with the rose petals to sounds of more cheers. Adam pulled her close to him and kissed her, hard and possessively. "You're mine," he growled in her ear, when he eventually pulled away.

"Yes, Master. I'm yours," she replied, just before he took her mouth again.

Adam then led Rachel over to a St. Andrew's Cross, which had been brought down from the playrooms upstairs. He took a pair of scissors from Luke and cut the flimsy dress so it fell around Rachel's feet, leaving her completely naked.

As he attached her to the cross, facing out toward the crowd, he spoke quietly in her ear. "We're going to do a public scene now. You may come whenever you like."

"Thank you, Master," she replied, her voice breathless with excitement. She'd never have believed before now that a public scene would turn her on so much, but it did. Her blood was buzzing as she watched Adam step back from the cross to inspect her. Every single person in the club was looking at her — naked and restrained. A powerful shudder ran through her body in response.

Adam then placed a blindfold over her eyes and kissed her softly, before stepping back, leaving her exposed and ready for him to use as he pleased.

The first thing she felt was his hot breath on her right breast just before he took her nipple into his mouth. It hardened instantly, and the shock sizzled all the way down to Rachel's pussy. She groaned as he sucked on it, just hard enough to cause a little pain, but not too much.

When her nipple felt as though it couldn't get any harder, or more sensitive, he pulled away. She waited excitedly for him to take her other nipple in his mouth, and screamed when, instead, he attached a clamp, pinching her solid nub painfully.

"Ow!" she cried. "It hurts, Master."

She heard him chuckle. "Go with the pain, Rachel. Accept it and you'll start to enjoy it. Remember?"

She did remember. He hadn't used these particular clamps since the night Amelia had given her that glorious orgasm. He must have been keeping them especially for tonight. He'd used less tortuous, adjustable ones several times since, but these clover clamps were in a different league. They bloody hurt.

Her body tensed as he sucked her left nipple to a hard peak. She knew this time what was coming. When the clamp bit into her, she screamed again as fresh pain seared her breast. But, just as before the pain did become bearable, and like before it didn't take long before the pain had turned into delicious pleasure pulsing down to her pussy.

Then Adam's breath brushed over her face and his lips took hers. His kiss was brutal and commanding, and took away any remaining control she might have had. She surrendered completely to that kiss, and knew that he had her exactly where he wanted her. It was liberating, and she let go of everything as she embraced her submission.

Then, Adam moved down her body, kissing her neck, breasts. He tugged on the chain linking the clamps and she screamed again as fresh pain tore through her abused nipples. Then he kissed her stomach, her belly button and her...

"Oh, yes!"

His teeth grazed the silky skin of her mound, at the same time as a finger gently pushed through the slick, hot folds to her pussy. Shit, she was so wet. His finger slipped effortlessly into her, and she arched her pelvis slightly to give him better access. Adam chuckled and pinched her clit, making her scream again.

Then something completely overwhelming happened. First, Adam's tongue licked her clit and he inserted another finger into her pussy, sending more hot waves of arousal coursing through her body. But at the same time, several hands started stroking her body—and they weren't Adam's.

Soft lips kissed her own. They tasted of vanilla lip gloss. Then another pair of lips nibbled her earlobe, the soft breath sending shivers down the back of her neck. Hands, more than one pair, then started stroking all over her body, whilst the two sets of lips continued kissing her all over. *Hmm, nice.* Someone took her nipple into their mouth and sucked hard while someone else licked the other nipple before caressing it with their lips. They were definitely women's lips, soft and sweet.

All this was going on whilst Adam sucked on her clit and fucked her pussy with his fingers. It was sensation overload. It was Heaven.

She guessed the two women were probably Amelia and Victoria, and her pussy heated at the thought of three people getting her off in front of the huge crowd. She groaned as Adam took her delicate clit between his teeth and pulled gently. Her knees buckled when one of the women pulled on the chain, sending electrifying pain shooting down to her clit in Adam's mouth.

She relaxed completely, stopped trying to work out what was coming next, but as soon as she did, she wished she hadn't because suddenly her world exploded.

Both the women removed a clamp at exactly the same time and took her tortured nipples into their mouths just as the blood rushed back. The agony was overwhelming and she screamed as the women sucked and licked at her tender nubs. At the same moment, Adam's fingers reached her G-spot and his tongue clamped onto her clit. The combination of sensations brought her to a screaming and shattering climax. Her pussy seemed to pulse forever, sending waves and waves of exquisite pleasure through her entire body.

Finally, the pain in her nipples calmed along with the aftershocks of her orgasm, and her body sagged on the cross in satiated glory.

The blindfold was removed and she slowly opened her eyes. Adam stood in front of her with Amelia and Victoria on either side of him.

"Thank you," she whispered, her voice sounding hoarse.

Both the women smiled and stepped silently away, while Adam reached up and released her from the cross. When he picked her up in his arms, the crowd cheered and Rachel buried her head in his chest as Adam carried her through to the aftercare lounge.

He laid her gently on the cushions and drew the curtain across so that it was just the two of them again.

"Did you enjoy that?" he asked, running his hand gently through her hair. The crown of thorns had been removed, although she had no idea when.

"Hmm," she murmured, smiling. "Yes, Sir. Thank you."

He chuckled and handed her a bottle of water. "Good. You've got a bit of time to recover and then we're going down to the dungeon. I'm going to make you come so many times tonight that you won't know what day it is."

She giggled. "I could never forget what day it is, Sir. It's the best day of my life."

"Mine too," murmured Adam, and kissed the top of her head. She snuggled against his hard, lean body and relaxed into his strong arms, holding her securely.

He didn't say anything for a while—they just sat in happy silence, enjoying each other's closeness.

"Come on," he said eventually, his voice regaining the powerful control which always weakened her knees. "We're going downstairs now. I've got a nice new flogger I want to use on you."

As if he'd flicked a switch, her body re-ignited with excitement as she realized she was going to get another treat.

* * * *

Rachel looked down at her body as Adam hoisted her arms up with some rope he'd looped through a hook in the ceiling. She felt restrained, helpless and oh, so very sexy.

Adam raised her arms until she was just about standing on tiptoes. She couldn't move, was completely at his mercy, and the moisture between her legs heated as he walked around her, inspecting her, flogger in hand.

She heard a scream then, and looked around to see where it had come from. She grinned when she saw Amelia, kneeling by Jack's feet, looking like she might be in big trouble. Jack was looking particularly mean, and she had a feeling that Amelia might be in for an interesting night.

Across the room, Mandy had Dawn bent over a spanking bench. Every time the riding crop hit her flesh, Dawn yelped and begged for more.

Rachel's eyes drifted over to a St. Andrew's Cross where Luke was expertly flogging Victoria with two large floggers simultaneously. She was groaning in ecstasy and obviously loving every minute of Luke's firm discipline.

Yes, all was well with the world. The room was full of sex, pain and pleasure, the smells now so familiar and the sounds so exciting. This was where she belonged, with these people who, like her, liked their sex with a bit of added spice.

Adam warmed her skin slowly with light even lashes, but it didn't take long before the strikes became harder and more intense. She threw her head to one side as the leather fronds landed on her tender breasts, and she moaned as her arousal intensified. She could feel the collar around her neck, a constant reminder that she now belonged to Adam, and she wouldn't have it any other way. Despite her past insecurities and Karen's bitter attempt at revenge, they'd made it this far and she knew that today was just the beginning of a long and beautiful journey.

"Get ready for your next orgasm, Rachel," he growled, as the leather flogger thudded against her pussy. "I want to hear you scream."

"Yes, Sir," she gasped, as another stroke kissed her warming flesh.

"I love you, Mrs Stone," he hissed, as he hit her again, only harder this time.

"I love you too, Mr Stone," she gasped, as the pain sent shivers of pleasure through her body. She loved him with all her heart and was so thankful that she could say the words out loud now, without fear, pain or guilt. She closed her eyes and felt herself drift into a cloud of euphoria as the second of the night's orgasms gripped her. Yes, this was where she belonged, she thought, as she drifted happily into subspace.

About the Author

Katy Swann is in her forties and lives near London, UK with her husband, three children and two cats.

When she isn't writing about strict, sexy Doms putting their strong-willed subs in their place, she likes to read about them. As well as writing, Katy spends her time trying to avoid the housework, keeping the kids from killing each other and drinking copious cups of coffee in the local coffee shop. Coffee and chocolate are the two things that keep her sane and focused, so they're often close by when she sits down to write.

To Love and Submit is her first erotic novel, which will be closely followed by To Love and Trust and To Love and Obey, which will complete the Boundaries trilogy.

Katy Swann loves to hear from readers. You can find her contact information, website details and author profile page at http://www.totallybound.com.

Totally Bound Publishing

Printed in Great Britain
by Amazon